THE
COUNTERFEIT
PRINCESS

THE

COUNTERFEIT PRINCESS

by Jane Resh Thomas

Clarion Books ⌾ New York

Clarion Books
a Houghton Mifflin Company imprint
215 Park Avenue South, New York, NY 10003
Copyright © 2005 by Jane Resh Thomas

The text was set in 11-point Amerigo.

www.houghtonmifflinbooks.com

Printed in the U.S.A.

Library of Congress Cataloging-in-Publication Data

Thomas, Jane Resh.
The counterfeit princess / by Jane Resh Thomas.
p. cm.
Summary: Vowing revenge when her parents are executed in 1553 by the Duke of
Northumberland, teenaged Iris becomes a messenger, spy, and stand-in for Princess
Elizabeth during the volatile political times surrounding Edward VI's death.
ISBN 0-395-93870-8
1. Great Britain—History—Tudors, 1485–1603—Juvenile fiction. [1. Great Britain—
History—Tudors, 1485–1603—Fiction. 2. Elizabeth I, Queen of England,
1533–1603—Fiction. 3. Messengers—Fiction. 4. Spies—Fiction. 5. Kings, queens,
rulers, etc.—Fiction. 6. Revenge—Fiction.] I. Title.
PZ7.T36695Cou 2005
[Fic]—dc22
                    2005008841

ISBN-13: 978-0-618-93870-6
ISBN-10: 0-618-93870-8

MP 10 9 8 7 6 5 4 3 2 1

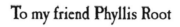

To my friend Phyllis Root

Acknowledgments

I am grateful to my editor of nearly thirty years, James Cross Giblin, his eye for drama and his ear for language; editor Lynne Polvino; art director Joann Hill; designer Kerry Martin; Phyllis Root, whose reading helped me find the heart; Pat Schmatz, for her unstinting encouragement; the Rainy Lake and Hayward writers; and the Oberholtzer Foundation, for providing the peace of Mallard Island, a well for thirsty writers.

ONE

The last time Iris ever saw her parents, they were bundling her into the cupboard behind the great walnut armoire in the library. She glimpsed her mother's blue gown and her father's kidskin slippers as the door swung shut and closed her up in the darkness.

The bright, blustery day had been ordinary until the king's men clattered across the courtyard at Linnetwood, the Earl of Bentham's country estate, just as Iris returned from a gallop in the fields. "Please, Thorpe!" she said, jumping down and handing the grizzled stable master the reins of her horse. "Will you rub down Shadow and put him away?" Excited to see emissaries from court visiting her home, she ran across the bricks behind the manor house and up the narrow stone servants' stairs, the shortest way to the gallery leading to her father's study.

She rushed through the open door. "Father, the king's men are in the courtyard!"

The earl stood so suddenly that his heavy carved chair teetered on two legs. "Simon," he said to his burly secretary, "fetch the countess at once."

Simon wiped ink from the tip of his quill pen. "What shall I do with the letters?"

"At once, Simon. Fetch the countess. I shall deal with the worst of the letters."

As Simon hastened out, Iris's father was already at the desk by the mullioned window, where the secretary had been writing. He hastily sorted through a pile of papers, placing some in a separate stack.

"Father," said Iris, "what is wrong?"

"They wear the king's livery, these men," he said, "but they do not represent him. King Edward is but a boy, and he is dying."

Iris's mother hurried in, followed by Simon and James, the estate treasurer. Iris's father handed the papers to James. "Burn these in the kitchen fire. Take the back way. Be quick."

The servant trotted out the door.

"Edward is a puppet," her father went on, "his strings pulled by the Duke of Northumberland and his underlings at court." He touched a panel in his desk. The panel sprang open, revealing a compartment Iris had never seen before.

"You're burning letters? Edmund—why?" asked Iris's mother. She had left her stitchery frame in such a hurry that she still held her needle, with its tail of embroidery floss, poised between forefinger and thumb.

Iris stared at the crimson thread as if it could answer her bewilderment.

Her father turned to her mother. "Northumberland's men have come for me, just as Cecil warned."

"Come for you? Cecil?" she said. "What has happened, Edmund?"

He removed his signet ring from his finger, took Iris's hand, and placed the ring on her thumb. "Whatever happens," he said, bending to look into her face, "keep this ring safe. It is proof of who you are."

"Whatever happens? But, Father—"

He turned his back on Iris, placed his leather journal in the desk's hidden compartment, and closed the panel.

Iris's mother poked the needle through the collar of her fur-lined cape and pulled Iris close. "We must hide her," she said.

With her father and mother's help, Simon slid the armoire away from the wall.

"Inside with you." Hastily kissing Iris on the cheek and smoothing her hair, Mother tucked her into a cupboard in the stone wall.

"No taper?" Iris wailed. "No light?"

"No time," her father said. "I hear them coming. Not a word until Simon lets you out."

The cupboard door shut. The armoire scraped back to its accustomed place. Suddenly shut up in total darkness on this golden day, Iris was uncertain the commotion was not a nightmare. A muffled shout sounded beyond the armoire, then the clatter of a scuffle. Something crashed. What was this ado about? Though Iris was not afraid in the unlit night-time stableyard or alone in her room at night, this darkness was more than an absence of light.

More scuffling came, but Simon would protect Mother and Father. Simon was a wall. He would stand between Father and Northumberland's men. And James the treasurer was a head taller than Mother—he would protect her.

A *shoosh* of metal on metal came, like a sword in a scabbard. "Leave us," said a strange man's voice.

Iris put her ear to a large crack in the cupboard door and strained to hear.

"Do as he says, James; go, Simon." Father was sending his protectors away.

"King Edward has need of you." This gruff voice was unfamiliar, too.

"You wear the king's insignia, but I know you're one of the duke's men," Father said. "Why has Northumberland sent his underlings for me?"

"The duke does the king's bidding," said the man.

"I would go anywhere for the king," said Father, "even to court."

"You, as well."

Who? The men were taking Father to London. Who else must go?

"Be quick, Countess."

"Put down your sword," Father demanded.

"Allow me to fetch my cloak." They were seizing Mother as well as Father.

"Where is your daughter?" This high-pitched third voice was rough.

"Oh, Iris," said Mother. "She would be sorry to miss a day at court, but surely the king wouldn't trouble himself with her."

"I regret to say," Father interrupted, "our Iris is visiting her Scottish cousins. What a pity for her to miss this opportunity."

"You're hurting me!" Mother again.

Furious at being shut up like a baby while something so terrible was happening, Iris struggled to open the door. No matter what Father had said, she must help. She leaned her back against the wall of the cupboard, placed her feet flat against the door, and pushed with all her might. She must get out. She pushed again and again, but the armoire would not budge.

Iris lay down exhausted on the floor.

No sounds came from the other side of the armoire.

She waited.

Nothing.

Now the silence was more fearsome than the hubbub had been. Iris screamed for her parents. She banged on the cupboard door until her knuckles bled and her fists were bruised. But no one responded. She huddled in the darkness, her dread growing with her hunger and the cold. What if Simon and James had been taken away as well? Only they knew where she was.

She fought against the armoire's weight again, until pain

tore one knee. Now she curled up in the corner, holding her throbbing knee to her chest and trembling as she turned Father's ring on her thumb. She would die here, starved and frozen. In a hundred years, somebody would find her and would wonder what had happened.

Iris must have fallen asleep, for the next thing she knew, the armoire scraped again across the flagstone floor, and the cupboard door opened. Her anger sputtered back to life as she emerged into further darkness. "Why have you left me here so long, Simon? Where have the men taken my parents? And why didn't you stop them?"

Simon helped her to her feet. "We dared not expose you until now," he said. "William Cecil has sent for you, Iris. You will go now with the greengrocer's man, along with the garlic and leeks and onions from the cellar. If Northumberland's hounds are set upon the cart, their noses will be so stunned with the reek of onions, they'll not care about you."

James tried to hustle Iris out of the room, but she squirmed out of his hands. "My parents, Simon! Where are they? James, tell me the worst."

Lucy Thorpe, who had suckled Father and had reared Iris as warmly as any grandmother, hurried into the room carrying a taper and took Iris's arm.

Now Iris was safe. Lucy would know what to do. "My parents, Lucy. Where have they gone?"

"Collect yourself, my girl," Lucy commanded. "This is no time for sniveling. They are gone to nothing good, you may be sure, and you will follow them, if we do not hurry."

"But—"

"No buts. No rebellion. Northumberland would kill you too, Iris. You must obey Simon, and quickly."

"Wait." Iris broke Lucy's grip. At the edge of the tapestry carpet by Father's desk lay Mother's cape amid scattered papers. Iris picked it up, caught a wisp of Mother's rosy scent, and touched the fox fur to her face for a moment before she tossed it over her shoulders.

Shaking her head, Lucy took Iris's arm again and steered her down the stairs as fast as she could move without falling, all the while brushing cobwebs from her hair, throwing a dark woolen shawl over the cape, and issuing further instructions.

"What will happen to Mother and Father? What will happen to me?"

"They must do the best they can, as they always have done. As for you, Iris, you must obey the vegetable man exactly," said Lucy. "He is not a laborer at all, but Lady Elizabeth's knight. He will protect you."

They stopped at the door to the stableyard. "We must wait here until they come for you," said Lucy.

Iris leaned against the doorjamb, shifting her weight off the painful knee. She knew, of course, that Lady Elizabeth was half sister to King Edward, like Lady Mary. They were all the children of King Henry VIII. When Henry died, he had left the throne of England to his nine-year-old son, Edward. If King Edward should die, Mary would be queen.

But what did Lady Elizabeth have to do with this day's trouble? Iris could make no sense of what was happening. Where had the Duke of Northumberland's men taken Mother and Father? And why had they not taught her that the duke was their enemy?

A servant startled Iris, taking her elbow and rushing her out the door. Now others were pushing her across the yard and into the stables. Then Thorpe took her in hand. The stables were lit by only one torch. In the dim light, Iris could not make out the face of the greengrocer's man, or cart driver, or knight, or whatever the fellow was. He and Thorpe lifted her into the cart and settled her among several large baskets.

"Head down, my darling," Thorpe said. "In come the onions with you. They shouldn't be too heavy." Iris sat on the floor of the cart, her legs straight out before her. Thorpe and others loaded a small basket of onions into her lap, then piled bags of leeks and turnips on her legs, and arranged loose turnips against her feet, and carrots that had wintered underground. They pulled the shawl over her head and piled in bags of garlic and other light things until she was fully covered. What could be so serious that she must hide? Iris breathed in the greenness that surrounded her.

"We shall be here when you return"—it was the voice of Lucy, who stood between the horse and the cart, right at Iris's head.

"Never fear, little maid," a man said from the seat at the front of the cart—the vegetable man, Lady Elizabeth's knight. Then came a cluck, the cart creaked and lurched, and Iris was on her way.

She tried to gather her thoughts. She had lost two mothers in one day, for her parents had allowed her to do as she chose, and Iris chose the company of Lucy. She chose the fields and the stables and the Thorpes' quarters rather than the drawing room elegance of the big house. This upbringing had been unusual for an aristocratic girl, to be sure, and Iris was grateful for her parents' leniency. She loved her wild rides on Shadow; she loved adventure. Now she had too much.

As the cart bumped along, Iris fretted. King Henry had married so many wives, her tutor had said, that people memorized a chant to keep all six of them straight: divorced; beheaded; died; divorced; beheaded; survived. Iris focused on the first three wives. Henry had divorced Catherine of Aragon, the mother of Mary, when he fell in love with Anne Boleyn, Elizabeth's mother. He beheaded Anne three years later to marry Jane Seymour, the mother of Edward.

Such confusion, history was; how could anybody keep it all straight? Now the betrayals that snarled the royal court had engulfed Iris's own family. King Edward was dying, Father had said. The vegetable carter was Elizabeth's knight, a stranger. He had taken control of her and was driving her who-knew-where. Her parents had been seized by men who would kill Iris if they could—kill her, *too,* Lucy had said.

Too? Had Lucy meant they would kill Mother and Father? Iris stretched under the weight of the vegetables to relieve a cramp in her thigh. Her hip bones and knee felt every bump in the road. The cart swayed from side to side, tipping her this way and that. The bag of leeks rolled in her lap. The basket of onions slid against her side and squeezed her against the bag of turnips. Nevertheless, the rocking and jostling lulled her. Exhausted by terror, she shifted again under her green burden and leaned her forehead against a hard and lumpy pillow—perhaps more turnips.

When she awoke, two men were unloading the cart inside a strange stable she had never seen before. Iris prepared herself for a fight, but then she recognized a voice; one of the men was the driver. He and his companion lifted her out and supported her as she flexed her knees and hips, for she was too stiff to stand alone. A woman with a curved beak of a nose plucked onion tops from Iris's dress and straightened the cape around her shoulders. Iris shook turnip dust from her hair and wiped the dirt from her face with the hem of the cape, while the woman hustled her across the torchlit stableyard to a stone manor house, another building she had never seen.

"What is this place?" she asked. "Where have you brought me? My mother and father—have you seen them?"

"'Tis the house of William Cecil," said the woman. "He shall explain."

She led Iris through oak-paneled rooms and left her standing in the library. There an austere man dressed all in black wool sat at a desk, writing a letter with a white goose quill. Light from a taper shone on his forehead. Iris stood across from him until he came to the end of his sentence. He dated the letter in bold black ink, *January 1553,* and put down the quill.

"Ah. There you are, my dear Iris," he said.

She looked down at her bloody knuckles and hid them in the folds of her skirt.

The man rubbed his hands across his fitted jerkin as he looked her up and down. Blue eyes glittered in his pale face. He brushed back his hair from his temples; though he was still quite young, the crown of his head was already bald. "You have been sent into my keeping," he said. "You no doubt wonder who I am."

"But my parents—"

"Yes, my dear. Your parents. They are foremost in my mind as well. I am very sorry to tell you that Northumberland has ordered them to the Tower."

The Tower of London, where so many had died. "What have they done, to be cast into the Tower?"

The king's ancient castle beside the River Thames was the site of royal ceremonies. It housed the crown jewels and armaments. It enclosed a church, St. Peter-in-Chains, and it was also a heavily guarded prison where enemies of the king served their sentences in cold cells, eventually to be executed. On the green within the Tower walls, at old King Henry's order, Anne Boleyn had knelt for a swordsman brought from France to cut off her head. What did the Tower have to do with Iris's parents?

Iris struggled to control her trembling. She would not allow this stranger to see her weak. "And who are you?"

"I? I am the faithful servant of the royal House of Tudor. Have your parents not told you what is happening at court?"

"The court is no business of mine."

"It is your business now." The man closed his eyes and put his hands to his head. "Princess Mary and Princess Elizabeth are the legal heirs to the throne. As King Edward approaches death, their danger grows. You know that Mary is Catholic?"

"No! I know nothing of anything! What has her religion to do with Mother and Father?"

"Never mind. It is enough for you to know that King Edward, Northumberland, and his supporters are Protestants. They will never let Mary become queen. Any friend of the princesses is endangered as well. Your parents were—*are*—their friends, you see."

Iris's head pounded. Mother and Father were Protestants, too. Why had they not educated her about these matters that their lives, and hers, depended upon? Until now, Iris had ignored royal antagonisms, even though she was fourteen years of age and her presence would soon be required at court. She grew restive while the man explained, but he went on.

"I am William Cecil, friend not only to Princess Elizabeth, but to your father and mother." He handed her a square of fine white linen for her nose.

The more this man Cecil explained, the more confused Iris grew. He had called Elizabeth by her rightful title, "Princess." Like Mother and Father, then, Cecil had not accepted her loss of rank after Anne Boleyn's death. Who was who? Who were friends? Who enemies? Who was Iris herself? With the loss of her home and her parents and Lucy and Thorpe, she had quite lost her bearings in the world.

Iris removed the ring from her thumb and held it out to William Cecil on her palm. "I am my father's daughter," she said. "He gave me his ring as proof."

"Yes," Cecil said, his voice catching. He placed the ring on her thumb again. "I well know who you are."

Iris wiped her eyes. "But what are you going to do with me? Can you save my father and mother?"

"We shall see. Pardon me another moment." Cecil dabbed at his eyes and nose and turned back to his letter. When he had finished writing, he poured sand over the inked words, curled the parchment to form a trough, and poured the sand back into its pewter pot. He folded the letter in thirds. Holding a stick of red wax in the candle flame, he dripped a molten blob onto the parchment. Then he pressed his ornate ring into the blob as it cooled.

"There," he said. "Take this letter with you. You can ride, I hear. I am sending you into the care of the woman who delivered you to me from the stable, Mrs. Pennefeather. She has many granddaughters; you will not be noticed at her house near London."

"London? But why? Why must I hide?"

Cecil barked a harsh laugh. "Why, indeed? You still don't understand, Iris. Northumberland would have your parents' estate. You are your father's heir. He would have you, too. We would not see you join your parents in the Tower."

At this reminder of the dreaded Tower, Iris shuddered.

TWO

he following day, Iris rode toward London with Mrs. Pennefeather and two male servants. The woman's house was secluded and simple, located on the outskirts of London and surrounded by extensive gardens, where Mrs. Pennefeather raised vegetables for the city market.

Most of the time, she ignored Iris. Her granddaughters came and went on brief visits, never staying long enough for Iris to befriend them. Nobody mentioned her parents. She spent her days in the gardens, longing for home, for Mother and Lucy. Nobody's daughter and nobody's friend, she felt neither dead nor alive.

Iris saw no more of William Cecil for a month. At last he came to visit her in February. He met Iris in the Pennefeather family's brick-walled flower garden, his face grave.

"What of my parents?"

Cecil looked at his feet. "I am sorry, Iris, but—"

Shrinking into her mother's fox-lined cape, Iris whirled away from him. "No! I do not want to listen to what you have to say." She pricked her finger on a rosebush and watched the blood bead.

"Iris, Northumberland—"

"I told you, I do not wish to hear."

"But you must, my girl. You must hear. You must weigh your future."

Must! Who was this stranger to tell her what she must do? Iris listened to a linnet in the tree overhead. This bird sang here just as its kinfolk did at Linnetwood.

Cecil waited.

At last Iris turned back to him. "Very well, then, if I *must*. I already guess what you would say, but speak."

"Your parents have died," said Cecil.

"Both of them? Father? Mother, too?" She could barely utter the words.

"Both. Northumberland executed your father. Your mother has died of the sweats."

Iris turned again and struck the rosebush with her open hand. She struck it again and again, until both hands were torn. Blood dripping from her fingers, she faced Cecil. "I shan't weep," she said. "I shall have revenge."

The corner of Cecil's mouth flickered. "They told me you were a firebrand." He sank onto an iron bench, staring into the distance for a time while Iris stood and waited.

As if he had decided something, he pointed her to another bench across from his own. "Sit."

Iris sat. She watched him. She waited for his words.

"We have need of messengers, from the court to Princess Elizabeth. A girl would not draw suspicion." He gave Iris a long, appraising look. "Are you up to the task?"

A princess could take revenge. Iris could not be a princess, herself, but Princess Elizabeth could do as she liked. If Iris served the princess as a messenger, she would come as near to power as she possibly could. "I can do anything for my parents' sake."

"Northumberland will attempt a coup when King Edward dies," Cecil said. "He will try, we think, to capture and imprison Princess Elizabeth and Princess Mary. You are familiar with the line of succession to the throne?"

"Of course! From King Edward to Princess Mary to Princess Elizabeth."

"Well, at least your father taught you something."

"But a coup? Only God determines the line of succession."

"Hmm. Yes. Unless Northumberland intervenes in God's will." Once again Cecil pinned her with hard eyes. "A messenger's life will be in peril, Iris."

"My parents are dead. What is life to me?"

"Does your obedience match your courage? They say you are headstrong."

Iris stood straighter, defying the question. Obstinacy, Lucy always warned, would be her ruin, and Mother and Father had worn her out with lectures about obedience. Now this stranger dressed in black would lecture for them.

"Are you?" Cecil asked again. "Many lives will depend upon you."

Iris hesitated. She would give anything now to obey her parents' wishes, every detail of them. "I shall obey."

"Very well. You shall remain here with Mrs. Pennefeather. She and others will train you in the trade of messenger and spy."

As the weeks went by, Iris no longer had time to idle outdoors, or even to cultivate Mrs. Pennefeather's gardens, for she studied from dawn to dusk. She learned pretense and stealth that she had never needed before. She learned to lie with a smile on her face. She learned to move through a crowd, her eyes straight ahead, as if oblivious, and yet to account for every person in that crowd, their numbers, their gender and class, the state of their nerves. She studied ink and charcoal sketches of Northumberland's men, and learned their names. She learned the servile manners of underlings, so different from the posture of her father's workers, in order to pass as one of them.

Her trainers taught her the arts of deceit, arts counter to the honesty Iris had learned at her mother's and Lucy's sides.

What had she come to, that people now were teaching her how to lie sincerely, how to say one thing and do another, how to be *not* herself. Indeed, as each day passed, she lost a little more of her sureness. She often consulted her father's ring to remember who she was.

Iris disguised herself and tested whether she could come as a stranger among Mrs. Pennefeather's servants, who by then knew her well; nobody recognized her. She posed as a beggar on the street by the gates of Greenwich Palace, another of the king's many houses, until she could identify the courtiers and doctors and craftsmen who came and went, and could distinguish the livery of each aristocratic household from all the others. She paid particular attention to the men wearing Northumberland's green and yellow clothing.

In early June, her trainers deemed Iris ready for her role as messenger. Mrs. Pennefeather told her she would be going to the Red Lion Inn, three miles from Hatfield Royal Palace, Princess Elizabeth's country estate.

"Speak to Cook and no other," said Mrs. Pennefeather. She handed Iris a jay's tail feather. "She will know you by this sign."

Iris pondered the feather as she prepared for her journey, wondering at the richness of even such a little thing. Though everything in her social world had turned bottom-up, the raspberries and the hum of honeybees, the wonder of feathers, all the familiar treasures of nature remained as they had always been.

In her sleeping room, Iris said good-bye to her mother's cape, nuzzling the fur that still carried a hint of her scent.

She replaced the cape in the cedar storage chest alongside her silken undergarments and her father's signet ring, tied in the corner of a handkerchief. Before she closed the door of the chest, though, she removed the needle with the crimson-floss tail that her mother had left in the cape's collar. Iris threaded the needle into the hem of her rough gown and poked the feather in and out through her coarsely woven collar.

Later that morning she rode out from London with a servant. They stopped at a crossroads near enough for Iris to see the Red Lion Inn's thatched roof across a narrow vale. She dismounted there, and walked the rest of the way alone. Over her shoulder, she carried a bundle containing one extra linen skirt and a change of scratchy underclothes.

The inn was a great pile of a timbered, whitewashed place, with a large stable and henhouse and other outbuildings standing in a semicircle behind it. Iris went around to the rear entry. Travelers were coming and going, stable boys currying horses, chambermaids beating rugs and feather pillows that hung on a line in the sun, other maids slopping the hogs in the sty and strewing grain in the yard for the hens. A brewer's carters unloaded six barrels of ale from a wagon pulled by oxen. The sun had begun its fall down the sky, in the lull between the noon and evening meals. Even in the yard, the fragrance of baking bread overwhelmed the stench from the stables.

Iris stood in the door of the kitchen, watching the hurly-burly within. At Linnetwood, Cook and Robinson, her assistant, always let Iris scrape cake batter from the bowl with her finger.

They baked pastry scraps, spread with jam and kept in a jar especially for her. Iris loved the warmth of a kitchen, but she had never labored in one, except to help Lucy for fun. A spasm of homesickness seized her, but she damped it down. She would endure anything to procure Elizabeth's help in her revenge.

With a clenched jaw, Iris approached a scullery maid who stood at a sink, scrubbing pots. "I want to see Cook about work."

The maid looked Iris over and shook the greasy dishwater off her chapped hands. Iris clasped her own hands behind her. They had never felt the burn of lye soap; they would give her away.

"That's 'er, stirrin' the soup. Name's Bartlesby." The maid tipped her head toward a heavy red-faced woman at the hearth. "Cook," she called. "A wench to see you."

Sweat dripped off Cook's nose and chin. On this hot afternoon in June, made hotter by the cookfire, she smelled something like the stables. "What do you want, girl?" She dipped her long-handled wooden spoon into the soup and sipped from it. "More thyme," she said, scooping a handful of herbs from a pot on a nearby shelf.

"Work," said Iris. "I want work." She removed the feather from her collar and casually handed it to Cook. The woman dropped it into the fireplace, where it flared for an instant in the coals.

"Can y' cook? Bake bread? Make pastries and meat pies? Walk six mile a day? Scrub floors?" No inkling of acknowledgment flickered in Cook's face. Had Iris come to the wrong place? Had she approached the wrong cook?

Iris nodded in answer to each question. "I can do any-thing you ask. What I don't know how to do, I can learn."

"Ho, ho," said Cook, standing straight and sizing up Iris. "You're sure of yourself, aren't you?"

Iris stood her ground and held Cook's eye.

"Well, you're a strapping lass. My egg girl hurt her leg. You can take 'er place. You'll be walking to Hatfield every morning with the delivery of eggs."

Just then a woman dressed in a severe black gown en-tered the kitchen. "Bartlesby," she said. "I employ the work-ers at the Red Lion."

"So you do, Ransom," said Cook, "the chambermaids and the serving girls—you're the housekeeper, they're yours. Not my kitchen maids." She shook her spoon at the woman. "You can hire all the Catholics you want for yourself—oh, yes, I know you favor them. The kitchen maids are mine."

Iris drew a shocked breath. So the fierce national argu-ment went on here, too. Iris had learned a great deal besides deception in the Pennefeather household. In this squabble between Bartlesby and Ransom, she recognized the echo of a conflict that had shaken England to its bones and threatened now to erupt again. Dissension had simmered throughout the country since King Henry severed the English church from the Roman more than twenty years before, in order to divorce Princess Mary's mother and marry Anne Boleyn. Nobody now admitted to being a Roman Catholic, lest King Edward's gov-ernment burn him to death.

Cecil had linked his fears of Northumberland to this rup-ture in the church. Fear of Mary's Catholicism, he had said, played a part in the plots at court. The Catholics resented the loss of the old religion, while the Protestants feared that Mary would become queen, restore the Roman church, and take revenge on those who had betrayed it.

For the moment, however, the argument in the kitchen had burned out. Iris became the egg girl. Every day at sunrise, she collected eggs from the Red Lion's coops for the use of the inn. At mid-morning, she walked to Princess Elizabeth's palace to deliver the extras to the kitchen. When she returned to the inn in mid-afternoon, she obeyed Cook, and Cook's assistant, and Cook's assistant's assistant, and the dishwashers and butchers and bakers and anybody else who had a mind to boss her: everybody, in short, who entered the kitchen.

When Iris's birthday came and she turned fifteen, nobody noticed. She wept that night on her bed of straw. Back in the kitchen the next morning, she scrubbed and kneaded and stirred and sliced. She sweated more in her first weeks at the Red Lion than she had sweated in her entire life before. Cook's odor no longer bothered Iris, for she carried a stink herself.

At every opportunity, Betty, the girl with greasy blond hair who washed the dishes in the dooryard sink from dawn to dusk, barked orders to Iris. "You there," she said, when Iris finished kneading bread and leaned on a table to catch her breath, "we've no room for layabouts. Get over here and scrub." Gall scalded Iris's throat. She longed to tell Betty to curtsy when she spoke to a lady, but she swallowed her anger. She obeyed Betty and everybody else, despite her aching back, and feet that burned, and bitterness that gnawed at her heart. She longed for her father's ring.

Alyce, a woman with a lazy eye, who swept the kitchen and the taproom, thrust the broom and a rag into Iris's hand when drunken roisterers became rough late one night. "*You* go clean up the puke," Alyce said. "You're so ugly, the sots'll never lay a hand on you." She cackled with a grin that revealed all her missing teeth.

Iris entered the taproom on her guard. A potbellied old man whose beard was rancid with last week's beef tallow pinched her bottom and breast. An overdressed young lord, doubtless on an errand from London to Hatfield, pulled her into his lap and lifted her rough gown, laughing at her undergarments. Once, she would have slapped these men and referred them to Thorpe for a whipping; now she smiled and kissed them on the cheek and escaped their fondling as best she could.

Iris had found a knife, dropped in the stableyard and overlooked, which she now carried at her waist, under her apron. As her character toughened, her appearance also changed. A kerchief hid her red curls, which were sodden anyway with sweat. The wisps that escaped from the scarf were plastered to her forehead and the back of her neck. A coarse rash reddened her hands, which were so chapped they cracked and bled, and her stained nails were broken.

In fact, Iris hardly knew herself, so shocking had been her transformation.

The journeys to Hatfield, which had seemed adventurous at first, now were mainly a walk through the countryside, rain or shine, the basket of eggs on her arm and no message at all in her hand. She enjoyed the journeys, even in the rain, for the air and the birds and the shade of the trees, but at the palace, she delivered the eggs to the Hatfield cook, who merely grunted, emptied the basket, and shooed Iris out the door. She had caught not a glimpse of Princess Elizabeth.

"May I but have a drink of water?" Iris once asked.

"There's the well," said Cook. "Serve yourself."

What a disappointment this life was—all drudgery and no excitement. Even if the princess was present in the palace, she was as distant from Iris as the stars.

One morning before dawn, Iris carried a candle and a basket to the dark henhouse behind the inn, to collect fresh eggs for breakfast, just as she had done every day for weeks. As she reached for the door latch, someone took her shoulder, saying, "Not a word," and thrust her inside the coop.

Iris threw off his hand and leapt away, in the same instant drawing the blade from under her apron. She held the knife at the level of the man's belly. "Who are you?"

The man held a finger to his lips and offered her a jay's feather with his other hand. Iris replaced the knife and put the feather in her pocket. The man was a courier from Cecil.

"Keep that feather safe," the man said in a low voice Iris could hardly hear. "The princess will not accept the letter without it."

"So I have been taught," said Iris.

The man's cloak was held high and his hat pulled low on his brow, so Iris could not see his face in the shadows. He removed a leather pouch from his tunic, and from the pouch a scrap that he handed to Iris. "Memorize the message," he said.

Iris unfolded the parchment. It had been scraped so many times, one message removed so another might be written, that it was nearly transparent. Poor people could not afford better writing materials. "Father dead," the message said. "Mother must stay to home and gather the flock. Keep sister close by until you hear from me." The letter was signed, "Your brother."

The courier spoke again. "Deliver this letter to the cook at Hatfield, along with your usual basket of eggs. Speak to nobody but Cook."

"But tell me—" Iris would know more.

The messenger interrupted her. "No chat, Iris."

So he knew her name.

"Without this letter, the princess will die." The messenger's voice was a raspy whisper now. "Northumberland means to marry his son Guildford to Jane Grey, Elizabeth's and Mary's cousin, and seize the throne. He would lure the princesses to London and imprison them there."

The man touched Iris's arm, as images of her parents and the Tower flashed across her mind. "Godspeed." He opened the door on its quiet leather hinges and merged with the darkness as quickly as he had appeared.

Iris stood in the fowl coop, catching her breath, breathing air heated by the hens' bodies, air ripe with the scent of their mash and feathers and dung. She read the letter again by the low light of the candle. Then, eyes closed, she silently recited the message back to herself, wrapped the feather inside the letter, and tucked it into her apron pocket. She would deliver the letter itself, as she had been taught, but, should it be confiscated, she could deliver it anyway from memory.

Iris slipped her hand under the hens one by one, brushing them off their straw nests when they squawked or pecked her, and removed their freshly laid eggs. The task completed, she returned to the kitchen, where she transferred some of the eggs into a large wooden bowl. Her hands trembled. Now that further adventure had arrived, she knew not whether to rejoice or to wish herself rescued from responsibility.

THREE

In an out-of-the-way corner of the kitchen, Iris read the letter again and made sure she had memorized it. Then she put it back in her apron pocket, remembering her instructions. Without this message, the man had said, the princess would die. Without the feather, the princess would not accept the letter. Iris would deliver it safely. Princess Elizabeth would survive, and Princess Mary would become queen. Iris would have her revenge on Northumberland. She would return to Linnetwood, and all would be well.

27

"Here, you—out of the way," said Cook. She pushed Iris aside with her porky hip. "The egg girl," she said to the other kitchen workers, "she thinks she's a lady, mooning about while others work." To Iris herself, she whispered, "Northumberland's men galloped by before daybreak. Godspeed." Grumbling, she turned again to her cookfire. Cook was an ally, then, after all; Iris had never been certain before.

Skillets clattered on the hearthstones as Cook fried the morning's ham and eggs. Oats that had been rolled and crushed with a stone boiled in a cauldron that hung from an iron rod above the fire. Serving maids came into the kitchen with trays of dirty dishes and went out with pitchers foamy with fresh, warm milk or ale. Breakfast for the journeying folk.

Trembling, Iris counted out the eggs for Hatfield into her own basket. Northumberland's men were abroad. They were always abroad, of course, but this day they had set secrecy aside. They would be stopping folk on the road. Looking for messengers like her. Intercepting letters bound for Hatfield. Nineteen, twenty, twenty-one eggs. Twenty-one white ones, their bony pallor the same color as the parchment letter. Three brown ones. Two dozen eggs, still warm from the hens.

Housekeeper Ransom bustled into the kitchen, puffed with her own importance, shaking her heavy ring of keys, to count the pewter and the knives.

"Hand me them eggs," said Cook. Iris crooked her free arm around the bowl containing the rest of the eggs and handed it over. "Lor', we've naught left, once the palace takes its cut. Ah, a few white ones still."

The eggs sizzled as Cook cracked them open with one

hand and spilled them into sizzling bacon grease. "'Tis bad luck to cook only brown eggs. They say the boy ate a brown egg."

"What boy?" asked Ransom.

"The king, of course."

"Brown egg, my eye," said the housekeeper, shaking her head. "King Edward is cursed for his Protestant ways." The Catholic housekeeper crossed herself, as if to keep the taint of false religion from her.

"Best guard your mouth," said Cook, "or you may find yourself arrested."

Poor King Edward. Gossips said he was dying, sickened with consumption. Others, the secret Catholics, said he was cursed for his Protestant beliefs. Some whispered that the Duke of Northumberland had poisoned him. Hungry for ever greater power, the duke had a motive; chief among the boy king's councilors, he had ample opportunity. Day and night, Iris had found, news of the king's court, truths and lies, half-truths and fantasies, came through this inn, where coaches and horsemen from London stopped for meals and sleep. Increasingly, their news accorded with Cecil's anxiety that Northumberland would attempt to seize the throne.

"Get a move on with that breakfast," called the innkeeper from the next room. "They'll soon sack the place, looking for food."

Slipping the handle of her basket over her arm, Iris stepped back into the stableyard, her cheek brushed by the roses that climbed the doorposts of the inn. Already the yard was alive with animals and men. Young grooms saddled the animals for the day's journey, and tied them to the rail along-side a manger filled with hay. The horses stood ready to go when both they and their riders had eaten their breakfast. Iris looked for a man who might be the courier, but he could have been any in the throng of travelers.

Iris threaded her way through the crowd, nimbly evading a horse's kick and a fat lout's fondling hands. Then she set off down the dirt road to deliver another day's eggs to the palace. Twenty-four eggs. Not many for a day at a royal house-hold where scores and sometimes hundreds of people worked, but these were not the only eggs the palace kitchen would receive. When the princess was in residence here at Hatfield, as she had been the better part of a year, the palace's own lands could not provide enough food. Farms and inns and village families for miles around made a living by supply-ing the palace's needs.

Without this letter, the princess will die.

Iris dawdled along the road, as William Cecil's trainers had taught her. Watchers must see no urgency. She picked up a baby sparrow that fluttered in a pool of dust, calling for its mother, its mouth agape, and set it in the grass at the edge of the road. She picked a purple blossom of spiderwort and pushed it through her knot of golden-red hair. Hot July hummed in the meadows and hedgerows.

A wagon approached behind her, driven by an old man and pulled by an ass, its long ears twitching. The wagon was rickety under an excessive load of dusty sacks, full of bulges that moved—chickens and rabbits, perhaps—and large baskets filled with new greens.

Iris walked on, occasionally stopping to peer through the tightly woven hedgerows at the sheep that browsed on the princess's lands. An oak forest grew beyond the meadows. Hundreds of ewes kept company with their lambs—mothers taking care of babies that were now grown big, too big for suckling anymore. They had nibbled the grass so short, it looked like green velvet, silvered with dew. A shepherd lolled near the edge of the lea, at a place where the hedgerow was sparse. He faced the road, though, rather than the flock. A shepherd or a spy? Iris resisted her need to look over her shoulder. The message she carried weighed heavy in her apron pocket. *Without this letter, the princess will die.* On she went, hurrying now, feeling eyes upon her.

As Iris neared the palace, the number of travelers on the road increased, riding horseback or driving wagons and carts filled with goods to be delivered at the palace gates. Men called greetings to their acquaintances and grunted orders to their beasts. Iris stayed near the edge of the track as the crowd grew; its progress slowed, and at last it stopped. Perhaps a tree had fallen across the road, but more than a week had passed since the last storm. No, maybe a wagon had overturned.

An ox bellowed, and a few horses whinnied. Protecting the basket in the circle of her arm, Iris climbed up a wagon wheel's spokes and stood on tiptoe to see what had caused the bottleneck ahead. Five men dressed in Northumberland's livery randomly searched the crowd. They jostled people afoot and inspected saddlebags and riders' pockets. One of the green-clad men stood in a wagon bed, slitting sacks with a long knife and rummaging through the vegetables that tumbled out.

Iris put one of the eggs in her apron pocket, atop the written message. The liveried man dragged the wagon driver from his seat. "What's this?" he said to the driver, pulling up the man's smock and cutting the straps of a money belt he wore at his waist. The duke's man shook the belt. Coins clattered within. "Now, what would a simple farmer be doing with a load o' coin like this?" The farmer fingered the bleeding cut in his belly.

Behind Iris, somebody pulled at her skirt. "Stand down." She turned to face a lad little older than her own fifteen years, who wore green and yellow.

"'Tis only the maid from the inn," said a woman with a basket on her arm. "She's but a girl."

The young man smirked. "The very sort I'd pick to carry a message. I'll just look over her . . . bags," he said. He cupped his hands around her breasts.

The woman flashed her leg and flounced her skirts, but the young man's attention to Iris did not waver.

Without this message, the princess will die.

Iris drew in a long breath and willed her trembling to stop. "Come see me on another day," she said flirtatiously, "when you are not so busy. I'll give you something especially sweet."

"I promise." The young man rummaged in Iris's basket.

Then he thrust his hand in her apron pocket and came up with the egg, watching her face without blinking, still grinning.

"Keeping one aside for yourself," he said. "Your master would not like it." He cracked the egg on Iris's head and poured it into his upturned mouth.

"Tie this 'un," said another of Northumberland's men, thrusting forward the bleeding farmer. "Take 'im forward with the others."

The lad kissed Iris on the lips and then went away to take the farmer in hand.

Iris feigned calm, while terror coursed through her. Northumberland would have her yet, and her own end would be the end of her father's line. No. Her enemy would not prevail. She would have him first. She edged between wagons and horses and oxen, working her way to the front of the crowd, hoping to find her way around the duke's men without their noticing her. Another man in livery seized her shoulder.

"The morning's eggs from the inn, m'lord," said Iris, flattering the rough fellow with a gentleman's title. She looked straight into his brown eyes and smiled, forcing herself to breathe slowly and deeply. The younger man's rough handling had broken two of the eggs. Their orange yolks had flowed over several of the rest. Iris saw then that the letter had been dislodged and protruded slightly from her apron pocket. She moved the basket to cover it.

"Leave the girl. We've bigger fish to fry," said another man. This glaring fellow scowled into Iris's face and sent her on her way with a toss of his shaggy head.

Iris hurried away from the checkpoint. If the duke's men

were openly searching people rather than merely spying, as they had for months, something must have changed.

Once Iris had rounded a curve in the road, she watched the hedgerow for an opening big enough to let her through, but it was planted and tended well to keep the sheep in. When she came to a stile, she scampered over it and headed across the lea toward the forest, hoping to hide herself there. She no longer trusted anyone—not even the sheep, she thought with a laugh. Ewes and half-grown lambs clambered to their feet as she approached, watched her, then bolted when she neared. Their movement would call attention to her, but the meadow had narrowed at that point, and soon she entered the woods.

This was the Old Forest, uncut from the beginning of time. Within the enormous oak trees' protection, making her way deeper into the shadows, Iris happened upon a well-trodden path that wound among arching brambles and through thickets of holly and thornapple. The shrubs' spurs grasped at her apron and scratched her arms, but she hurried on nevertheless, turning this way and that to release herself.

The path led her to the edge of the woods, where she stopped to assess the risk. In the distance, the redbrick palace stood warm in the sun, its three wings wrapped around a courtyard at the back. Behind the palace, the goose girl directed her flock of ducks and geese with a long, flexible willow wand, prodding them toward deeper, greener grass. Two girls in aprons came from the byre, carrying full buckets on the broad wooden yokes across their shoulders. They set the buckets down by the dairy, where other milkmaids stood churning. The wind carried their song so well, Iris recognized it: "Come, butter, come," the churning song she had heard all her life. Dairymaids had sung it at the inn this very morning; in the dairy of William Cecil, her rescuer; in the winter kitchen at Linnetwood, in years past.

"Come, butter, come." Now Iris chanted the words to herself. She had learned it when servants taught her to churn. In those days she could churn or not, as she chose. Now she did Cook's bidding, whether she chose or not. Choice, she had been bitter to learn, was a privilege. She crouched here in Elizabeth's wood, taking nourishment from hate. She served herself as well as the princess. Whatever the danger, she would destroy Northumberland.

Still Iris watched, alert to signs of change. Elsewhere in the yard, around the outbuildings at the side of the palace, young pigs suckled at their mothers' bellies. Sawyers unloaded logs from one of several heavily laden carts and cut them into firewood of a size to be carried to the palace hearths. A stable boy released the herd of golden cows into the field, where they followed their leader to better pastures.

Every person tended to work, calm, unhurried, never glancing about, attentive to only the everyday business at hand. The horses did not mill around or tremble. Every cow and goose and pig behaved as it always did. News of whatever was happening at King Edward's court obviously had not yet reached Hatfield Royal Palace.

Would the message Iris was bringing to Elizabeth disturb this placid life?

FOUR

ris emerged from the woods to cross the meadow, climbed over a stile into the workyard, and hurried then to the kitchen door. Baker's pulled loaves of fresh-baked bread from the oven. Iris's empty stomach growled at the delicious aroma.

"Iris," said one of the scullions, "what kept you so late?"

"The duke's men," said Iris. "They're stopping everybody on the road, but they wouldn't say why. What do you suppose it is?"

Two maids glanced at each other like conspirators as the darker of them tied her hair back with a ragged strip of black cloth. Iris would watch that pair in the future.

"Never you mind," said the Hatfield cook. "'Tis no concern of the likes of you. Here. Tend to your business."

Cook pulled at Iris's arm in her usual rough way. She yanked her to the wooden box cupboard, where food was kept cold by a stream of icy spring water underneath. A stone-lined sluice directed the stream through the kitchen wall and back out to the yard to fill the troughs with ever fresh water for the chickens and cows.

With her sleeve, Cook wiped her brow, already wet from her labor at the hearth. She opened the cold-cupboard's latched door and counted out the eggs into a bowl on a high shelf.

Iris handed her the jay's feather. Cook nodded. "You broke some," she said, loud enough for the others to hear.

"The duke's men were rough," said Iris.

As if continuing to scold, Cook mumbled, "Thank the Lord you're safe."

Iris removed the letter from her apron pocket.

Cook wiped with her own apron at the yolk that had drib-bled across the parchment and dried. The letter was not sealed, for it must seem ordinary. Letters of any kind were un-usual enough, in this day when few people besides priests and kings could read.

"You're to take this to Herself," said Cook. "She wants to see you." She removed the wilted flower from Iris's hair and replaced it with the jay's feather.

"Herself?" Iris gave her dirty apron to Cook and put the

letter in her shoe. Whom did Cook mean? One of Elizabeth's ladies? After her weeks in the Lion's kitchen, Iris would hardly know how to act.

"Go around to the front. She's reading in the knot garden," said Cook. She glanced out the kitchen's open door. "Sun today could knock your eye out. Look under the rose arbor." She closed the cupboard. "Go along," she said, her voice growing louder as she spoke. "I've enough to do, without cossetting clumsy egg girls." She made a sweeping gesture toward Iris. "Out!"

As she hurried around the side of the great brick palace, Iris silently rehearsed the letter she had memorized. "Father dead. Mother must stay to home and gather the flock. Keep sister close by until you hear from me. Your brother." She fretted at her hair and fussed to straighten her skirts.

The bench in the knot garden at the front of the palace was empty, but Iris delighted to see the place Hatfield's gardeners had made famous. Elizabeth's stepmother, Katherine Parr, her father's sixth wife, had planned this garden and sometimes tended it herself. Iris patted the hoof of a stag she passed, one of the beautifully carved and brightly painted animals that stood at intersections in the graveled paths. A lion and a unicorn from old King Henry's time stood on their hind legs at the center of the garden, the lion covered with gold leaf, and the unicorn with silver that shone too brightly in the sun to be viewed for more than an instant. They wore ruby and white silken ribbons that the wind floated and tangled about their necks. Iris smiled at a carved brown bear, its neck encircled by a wreath painted green and gold and red.

Sharply trimmed privet hedges crossed each other to create geometric shapes, like the Celtic borders in her father's illuminated manuscripts. Though Northumberland had confiscated them, Iris remembered the manuscripts and books and house and lands and all. The duke had stolen much else as well. Now, if William Cecil and the courier were correct, he intended to pirate the throne itself.

Iris made her way slowly down the graveled paths of the knot garden. The plants that grew within the hedged squares and diamonds and circles were all the finest flowers of the realm, it was said, and many new ones besides, brought back to England by explorers who had sailed down the coast of Africa. Seeing nobody except gardeners on their hands and knees, clipping hedges and cultivating flower beds, Iris walked toward the colonnaded arbor. It supported a profusion of white roses and led to the front gate, where noble visitors entered the palace grounds. Her own father and mother had doubtless entered there.

Iris stood inside the arbor, blinking in the green darkness after the brilliant sunlight of the garden. As she regained her sight, she made out a figure fifty feet away, midway down the long narrow room the roses created, with a little dog lying at her feet, watching. The figure was a woman. She sat on an ornate iron bench, her back to Iris. Was this person "Herself" or another highly placed companion, perhaps Kate Ashley, Elizabeth's governess from childhood and still her closest servant? Although Iris, suddenly shy, tiptoed down the path toward the bench, the gravel underfoot gave her away. Yet the woman did not turn or even look up. Perhaps she had nodded off.

The heady scent of roses bore Iris along. When she was near enough to touch the bench, unable to tolerate the tension another instant, she spoke at last. "Madam—" She cleared her throat and spoke again in a louder voice. "Madam, Cook sent me with a letter."

"Well?" replied the woman. "Bring it to me."

"One moment." Iris turned toward the roses at her side, her face hot, and removed the letter from her shoe.

"Don't keep me waiting," said the lady.

The day was hot, and the parchment had absorbed sweat from Iris's foot. Iris put the letter to her nose. Nothing offensive, she found, but only the scent of damp parchment. Very well. She must hand it over, damp or no.

The dog stretched and came to meet her. Iris knelt for a moment to pet him, then gathered her courage and went around the bench. Sitting there in a plain russet gown was a young woman with a halo of curly red-gold hair that escaped the knot at her nape. When she looked up from her book, Iris recognized her from portraits—the pale skin and deep-set green-and-hazel eyes, the long, narrow face and nose, the serious expression.

The woman was Princess Elizabeth herself.

Iris fell to her knees. Propriety demanded she curtsy, but her legs would not support her, so she knelt.

The princess closed her book. Iris glimpsed the title, *The Canterbury Tales,* embossed on the brown leather cover and touched with gold.

"Enough groveling. Get up."

Trembling, Iris stood. She fumbled in her hair for the jay

feather, which she handed to the princess. How annoying that weeks in the scullery had made her awkward with a highborn woman.

"So you are Bentham's daughter. He used to dandle me on his knee when I was but a tot. He was the best of my father's friends." She closed her eyes for an instant. "After my mother's death, when none else would visit me, though I was but a blameless child, he and your mother came to stay for a time. They comforted me until they died themselves." She looked deeply into Iris's face. "Yes. I see your father in your eyes. I see your mother in you, too—her hair was pretty, like yours."

Iris nodded. Her mother's hair and her own, she saw now, were very similar in color and texture to Elizabeth's.

"Do you remember me?" Elizabeth asked.

"Now that I have seen your eyes," said Iris. "Nobody could forget your eyes, your Highness."

"No 'Highness' here, anymore. 'My lady' will do," said Elizabeth. "I, like you, have come down in the world. You have a letter for me."

"'Tis damp from my shoe," Iris said.

"Never mind. Here. Sit by me." The princess pointed at the dog. "Skye is his name. He alone I can truly trust." She took the letter, opened it, and read. Then she dropped the parchment in her lap and covered her eyes with her hands, while robins flitted and sang among the roses. After a moment, she pulled her shoulders back and turned to Iris. "Thank you. You have risked your life, and I shan't forget."

Iris sat on the edge of the bench, her back as straight as

she could make it, her hands folded in her lap. She had indeed risked her life, but she had done so for herself as much as for the princess. If Iris herself were a princess, she would make better use of her time than reading in the garden. She would raise an army; she would save the condemned.

Princess Elizabeth pointed at the line in the letter that said, "Father dead." "The king—my brother—is dead," she said, and cleared her throat. "'Mother'—I am 'Mother'—'must stay to home' and gather my flock. I shall stay here with my knights. You are 'sister.' You shall remain here with me."

"Stay? For how long? Cook expects me back at the Lion in time to scrub the kettles." Iris was dumbstruck. As suddenly as Northumberland had orphaned her, stripped away her inheritance and paupered her, Princess Elizabeth was raising her up again.

"For as long as I shall need you."

Iris would work in the household of the princess. Someday Northumberland might visit, and Iris would have her revenge.

"You and I are both orphans," Elizabeth went on. "My mother died when I was but a child of three years."

Iris stared at Elizabeth, now a young woman approaching the age of twenty, while Elizabeth stared down the alley of roses toward the gate and a thousand yards beyond. With her brother, King Edward, dead, she was rightful heir to the throne after Mary. As Iris had learned to her sorrow, however, Northumberland would take what he wanted. He would have Hatfield, as he had taken Linnetwood. Life at this royal palace would not be peaceful.

Hoofbeats approached. The horse pulled up at the gate. A rider dressed in Northumberland's green and yellow dismounted. The sentries let him through the gate, accompanied by three of Elizabeth's men, all of them with hands on the pommels of their swords or knives. The men approached down the long walk, their boots crushing the gravel and throwing up little puffs of dust.

Iris curtsied to the green man. Skye growled and nipped his ankle. He kicked the dog away and elbowed Iris aside; she fell onto the path. How imperious he was, and how Iris had come down in the world's eyes—she would never accustom herself to servitude.

Elizabeth picked up Skye and petted him in her lap. "A man who wished me well would treat my companions kindly. Come sit beside me, Iris."

Iris joined Elizabeth on the bench. Northumberland's man knelt on one knee, an exaggerated, obsequious courtesy. "A letter from the duke."

The parchment was sealed with a hardened blob of red wax, imprinted with King Edward's crest.

"Your knife," said Elizabeth to the messenger. She left the man kneeling.

He handed her his knife, hilt foremost. She slit the letter's flap and laid the knife in her lap. When she had read the message, she gave the letter, still open, to Iris.

"My Lady Elizabeth," Northumberland had written. "His Majesty, King Edward VI, has rallied. He asks for the presence of his sisters at his bedside, but he is too ill to write to you in his own hand. Lady Mary, your sister, has already arrived.

Your faithful servant, John Dudley, Duke of Northumberland."

"'Tis my brother's seal and Northumberland's handwriting, and we know what a faithful subject he has always been." Princess Elizabeth allowed the irony to hang in the air a moment. "Thank the duke. We shall leave on the morrow for London."

Princess Elizabeth stood, the knife in her hand, and Iris clambered to her feet beside her. The two young women towered over the kneeling messenger while the dog growled at him. What a pleasant sensation, Iris thought. This small comeuppance betokened the great one that would befall the duke himself one day.

"You may go," said Elizabeth brusquely, turning her back on the messenger.

One of the Hatfield men accompanied Northumberland's man back to the gate. The other two moved away a few steps, but they stayed, awaiting a word from Elizabeth. Each of them wore an embroidered "E" on his jerkin.

"Curse Northumberland's eyes!" said Princess Elizabeth. "He would murder us both, Mary and me, and take the throne himself. Or give it to his son."

"May I speak?" said one of Elizabeth's guards, a man with deeply tanned skin and black eyes.

"Of course, Jeremy."

"The courier told me the duke is marrying his son Guildford to Lady Jane Grey."

Taking the knife by its point, Elizabeth hurled it into the ground at her feet. It shuddered in the earth. "In fact, Guildford has already married my cousin Jane, days ago, and

two more of Northumberland's pups have married my relatives to be near the throne when I am dead. Robin Dudley sent
me word yesterday."

Robert Dudley? Northumberland's son? Iris strained to
understand. "But, my lady, why does Robert Dudley—"

"Report his father's doings to me?" Elizabeth laughed.
"You have been too sheltered, Iris. There is no end of treachery in this world. Robin and I have been friends since our
ninth year. We played together as children. Perhaps he thinks,
when I am queen, he shall be king."

Elizabeth's men still waited nearby. "What do you wish to
do?" said one.

Elizabeth did not ponder an instant. "Prepare to go to
London."

The man scowled. "Surely you would not walk into
Northumberland's trap, my lady."

"Certainly not, but I would have him think so."

FIVE

silent maid led Iris through room after room. Knights and other gentlemen were everywhere, leaning on walls or lounging on benches, talking in agitation, their feet a-stutter on the reed mats that covered the floors. In the rooms where the gentlemen had not congregated, servants whispered as they polished pewter candlesticks, cleaned hearths, and swept and dusted. Everything was shabby. Iris passed two middle-aged ladies, whispering; they glanced sidelong at her, their faces tight. At last, the maid ushered Iris through an archway into a space the size of her mother's largest closet. The narrow bed that stood in the corner would be a luxury after the thin straw pallets at the inn.

The maid tied back the drape at the window. "If you need something, my lady, you need only ask," she said. "Call out. Somebody will come." She backed out of the room.

"My lady." For months, Iris had been the one to curtsy and bow her head and look at the floor and listen to orders. She had answered the calls and done the bidding of others. The maid's respect half embarrassed her now. She looked out the mullioned window to see where in the palace she was. Below, more flower gardens extended beyond the alley of roses. She must be in the left wing of the palace. She sat down on the edge of a chair, beside a table where a bowl of soup steamed. A plate of cold beef and cheese and warm buttered bread lay under a cloth. Fine white bread. Iris had eaten none but coarse oat bread in all her months at the inn.

As she ate a buttered slab, her thoughts tumbled over each other. Her second-best clothes were at the inn—another sashed smock, dyed blue with indigo like this one, nothing suitable for the household of a princess. Cook would think Iris had run off and deserted Elizabeth's cause, now that the danger had deepened. Someone else would have to gather the eggs at the Red Lion tomorrow morning.

Iris imagined herself at court, dressed in satin and velvet, dancing with the foremost men of the realm. Soon, though, she fell to fretting. When the princess no longer needed her help, what would become of her? And if Northumberland should capture Princess Elizabeth, what of her royal house-hold? The duke's courier had seen Iris here. No one had paid enough attention to her, a mere girl, to associate her with the Earl of Bentham, her father, but she could never live in the open while Northumberland held power. She gulped watered ale from a goblet, surprised by her thirst.

Suddenly exhausted, Iris left the soup and the beef un-touched. She brushed off her skirts with her hands. Dust that had been invisible on the blue cloth rose around her. She lay down on the counterpane that covered the narrow bed, and sank into the soft featherbed that lay atop the wool-stuffed mattress.

Unable to rest, she got up again, pulled the chair to the window, and stared out beyond the flower gardens to the road that led to London. So Guildford Dudley had already married Lady Jane Grey. Northumberland was exploiting the complex web of royal relationships. Like Mary and Elizabeth, Lady Jane was a Tudor, the daughter of King Henry's niece. As cousin to King Edward and the princesses, Jane Grey stood well forward in the line of succession.

Now Iris understood. Northumberland was devious. He could argue, as King Henry himself had done, that Henry's marriages to his first two wives had been illegitimate; thus, he would say, Mary and Elizabeth were bastards, while Jane Grey's claim to the throne was pure. Northumberland would control Queen Jane as he had manipulated King Edward, and thus would he explain his theft of power.

Iris sighed. Far from relieving anxiety, her growing understanding of the duke's motives terrified her. If Northumberland won, he might imprison Elizabeth's friends. He might even execute them. From the edges of court life at Linnetwood, she had entered the whirlwind now. Only one place would be more dangerous than Hatfield Royal Palace: the household of Princess Mary.

A knock at the door startled Iris. She leapt to her feet. A smiling woman of middle years opened the door. Her cheeks and large nose were shiny with scrubbing, and her black, observant eyes were kind. "I am Katherine Ashley," she said. She took Iris's hand and kissed it. "I know you carried Cecil's letter. Thank you for helping my dear Elizabeth."

Iris bowed her head. This woman assumed Iris's loyalty was selfless. Had she never thought that the daughter of the Benthams might want revenge?

Mrs. Ashley went on. "I have served the princess since she lost her milk teeth. She is all the world to me."

This woman who had been a second mother to Elizabeth was wrong. Iris cared about the princess's fate, indeed she did—but Princess Elizabeth's life or death was nothing to her beside the memory of her parents. Images of her father's raven-stripped skull, looking down on London Bridge, haunted her dreams and darkened her days. Should God answer her prayer for an opportunity, she would kill Northumberland herself.

"My lady? My lady?" Mrs. Ashley gently tugged at Iris's sleeve. "You are well?"

"Yes," said Iris. "I'm as well as I have been in months. What is it?"

"Princess Elizabeth has asked me to fetch you after you have eaten."

Iris took one more hurried bite of buttered bread. Then she followed Katherine Ashley. They proceeded farther along the row of connected rooms toward the back of the palace. Through another bedroom. A reception room. A dining room. Mrs. Ashley knocked gently at the side of a doorway, waited for Iris to precede her, and left her there in the sitting room with Princess Elizabeth and the three knights from the rose arbor. The men stood and bowed a courtesy. Elizabeth moved a bishop on the board where she and one of the men, the one she had called Jeremy, had been playing chess. Then she fixed Iris with those cat's eyes that were so intense, they might have burned through iron.

Iris curtsied, glancing around her at the princess's plain wooden furnishings and the faded, sooty tapestries on the walls. The scarlet draperies at the windows were ragged at the edges. The oak floor, like all the others in the palace, was covered with rush mats. On the back of one chair were carved the lion and the unicorn, the Tudor coat of arms.

"Yes," said Elizabeth, following Iris's glance. "We live simply. What we have is what was here in my father's day, when I was a baby and Hatfield was his hunting lodge. The king my brother has afforded us little money for expenses." The dog Skye lay beside her on the bench, licking her hand. "Unlike my sister Mary, I prefer simplicity anyway."

Iris had seen Princess Mary once at Linnetwood; she was a small, gaunt woman with a raspy, masculine voice. Seventeen years Elizabeth's elder, she had worn black velvet, richly decorated with pearls and gold embroidery, with ropes of pearls around her neck and gold on every finger. People associated luxury with Roman Catholics like Princess Mary. Elizabeth made a silent statement of her Protestant beliefs through the plainness of her attire. Today she wore no jewelry but amber drops in her ears; only the jay's feather Iris had given her adorned her russet gown. She had threaded the feather through the fine linen fabric.

"Down now, Skye," said Princess Elizabeth, moving the little dog to the floor.

She turned to Iris. "I have asked you here for a reason, of course. Sit there." She pointed at a walnut bench. The blue cushions were worked in a stitched design of falcons.

Iris sat and waited with her hands clasped to control her agitation. She had been brave enough today, facing Northumberland's men, risking her life to deliver a crucial message. The thought of the young man fumbling at the egg in her apron pocket still made her tremble. Perhaps now an opportunity for revenge would present itself. If Northumberland fell and Elizabeth lived, she might invite Iris to join this royal household. Its men would protect her. She would see the princess every day.

Iris would join the rebellion against Northumberland, and, when he was destroyed, she would go with Elizabeth to Queen Mary's court and see the duke beheaded. Or Iris herself would find a way to poison him. Everywhere Elizabeth went, people would watch Iris and envy her position, and in a few weeks she would return to Linnetwood, its mistress.

The princess interrupted Iris's daydream. "We have assured the duke that we will leave immediately for London, as you heard, Iris. He must see us traveling, yet we must not leave the relative safety of the palace." The princess paused, while Iris took in her words.

Such confusion. The princess must be seen traveling, but must remain at the palace.

"If we try to escape, Northumberland's men will attack our company and capture us on the road," said Elizabeth, watching Iris as she spoke. "But if we proceed naïvely, he may wait for me to present myself at court, where he could seize me and imprison me in the Tower, out of sight. The people know nothing of my plight. I would be dead before they even knew Northumberland had captured the throne."

The princess turned to the eldest of the knights. "Go on, Edgerton," she said. "Explain our plan."

"On the other hand, if Princess Elizabeth stays at Hatfield, we can put up a strong defense here," the man called Edgerton said. "From today, as fast as horses can gallop, the people of England will learn that Northumberland has betrayed the crown."

Remembering the fate of her parents, Iris tried to hide her pessimism. Whichever choice Elizabeth made, whether she stayed at Hatfield or fled or answered the summons to London, Northumberland would have her.

"We shall play Northumberland's game for time," the princess went on. "Time is all we need. Given time, Mary's forces will unseat the duke, and Guildford and Jane, those poor puppets. Given time enough, Mary shall be queen."

Iris listened, watching Elizabeth's face, searching the faces of her men, who returned Iris's gaze with an intensity that frightened her. She doubted that time alone would be enough. Elizabeth's red-haired head would join Father's on London Bridge. Perhaps Iris's own red head would join them. Why should they tell Iris these hopeless plans?

"I make no demands," said Princess Elizabeth. "My servants and friends may leave now, if they wish, with no regrets. Or they may stay. My sister grows old—she is already thirty-six years of age, and she is unwell. When I am queen, Iris, I shall repay my loyal servants."

Shivering, Iris clasped her arms around herself.

"I believe Northumberland would not hurt my household, but only me," said the princess. "Nevertheless, you all must decide for yourselves whether to stay or leave."

She gestured at another of the men. "Go on, Bartlett."

Iris pulled at a loose thread in her skirt and stroked the cloth between her fingers. Her heart rejoiced in this opportunity to help bring Northumberland down, but fear overwhelmed her pleasure. She wanted to be the egg girl again at the Red Lion, to follow Cook's orders, to pour ale from cool jugs into drunken travelers' mugs. She would marry the cowherd and rear a family of children. Would to God she might go deaf and hear nothing that Bartlett or anybody else had to say.

Bartlett had already begun to speak. ". . . play for time," he was saying. "The Duke of Northumberland—my behind! John Dudley he was, and John Dudley he is yet, a traitor like his father. The people hate him."

The chess player—Jeremy—had said nothing, but he watched Iris with sizzling eyes. Now he leaned forward until she could smell the wine on his breath. "At a tavern in London two nights ago, in the shadow of Richmond Palace, a drunk-ard fashioned a wee Dudley doll with a bit of straw and string and his handkerchief, and cast him into the fire. A hurrah went up that I feared might raise John Dudley himself from his bed at Richmond."

The princess laughed.

"Small troops of soldiers have gathered at farms all around London, and even within the gates, preparing to resist Northumberland at the king's death," the third man went on. "Mary set out for court, but a London goldsmith brought her the news of Edward. She has fled to the eastern counties. If need be, she'll escape to the Low Countries."

Iris felt a surge of pride in her countrymen. She quelled her fear. What would her own death matter now, when every-thing she treasured had been taken, all but the love of Thorpe and Lucy, her second family at Linnetwood?

"Ah," said Princess Elizabeth, staring out the window. "Do not speak of my brother's death." She was silent, pluck-ing at her throat with fingers of astonishing length and grace.

The men held their tongues and waited. When she turned back to Iris, her eyes glistened, but she went on in a strong voice that betrayed no further grief or fear. "Your mission will be very dangerous. The decision is yours." Then Elizabeth sat back as if she didn't care, weighing Iris, her eyebrow cocked, a small smile at the corner of her mouth. She raised her hand to her chin and waited, silent. Iris felt like prey.

"What mission? What decision?" said Iris. "What do you want of me?"

"Surely you must have noticed you resemble me, Iris," said the princess. "Your stature . . . your pale skin. Your hair is the very color of mine. With a scarf at your throat and about your face . . ."

"We want you to pose as the princess and dally on the road to London," said Edgerton. "Put Northumberland to sleep, thinking his plot has lured the princess to court. Divert his attention until we see what Mary does. Before you ever arrive in London, I'll wager, Northumberland's head will be in a basket."

"The duke will behead *me,* as he did my father." Iris put her face in her hands.

"A retinue of knights will travel with you," said Edgerton, "protecting you, just as if you were the princess."

Iris reflected as rage rose in her throat. She had done William Cecil's bidding for months. She had even obeyed willingly, despite the danger, grateful for his kindness. She was glad to resist Northumberland, glad indeed to aid the princess, who had suffered the betrayal of so many others. Now these people she had served would send her into the lion's mouth. Iris held Princess Elizabeth's gaze. Neither would blink or look away.

At last, Elizabeth spoke. "I knew your parents well. Northumberland seized them because they were my strongest support, and they opposed him. You can continue their mission. You can stop the tyrant."

Now Princess Elizabeth was manipulating her, as Northumberland had manipulated King Edward. A mere mention of her parents could stir Iris to action. Yet Princess

Elizabeth's account was true. Iris's role as messenger had been small, but here was a greater role. Her actions could bring the Duke of Northumberland to his death.

"If he should capture you, I shall present myself in exchange for your freedom," said Princess Elizabeth in a low voice. "I promise it."

Everything in Iris clamored for her to run, yet she must not panic. She could leave Hatfield, walk north to the isolation of the lakes, or west to the wilds of Wales, and melt into the countryside in some tiny village where nobody cared where she came from. She had lived successfully as a servant for many weeks now; she could do so the rest of her life, though she would live as a coward. Or, as she had longed to do, she could seize this opportunity to help others avenge her parents' death. She could put her life in Elizabeth's hands, even though the princess was very unlikely to survive the turmoil of this week, let alone ever ascend to the throne and reward her faithful servants.

"Very well." Iris drew in a quavering breath. "I shall do as you ask. Not for you alone, your Highness. For my mother and my father. For myself."

"Those are good reasons, too." Princess Elizabeth stood, took Iris's right hand in her own, and raised them high over their heads. "John Dudley, into the fire!" she said.

Iris raised her other hand in a fist. "Amen!"

six

ris sat at the window of her tiny bedchamber, wearing somebody else's nightdress and somebody else's plain gray gown. The somebody-else's clothing she wore was nothing new to her, of course, for she had not been herself since leaving Linnetwood. As she looked out over the dew-drenched garden, a serving maid, her dark hair caught back with a ragged strip of black cloth, brought breakfast on a tray. Iris knew her—one of the conspiratorial girls from the kitchen yesterday. Iris watched her lay the pewter

dishes out on a clean white cloth and then remove the covers from the food.

"'Tis the same as my lady ate this day," said the girl, "but that she picks at her food like the birds in the wood."

"She is awake already? I imagined a princess could sleep until noon."

"She could, if she would. She sleeps but little, too," said the maid. "Especially now. She rises early anyway, and today, you know, she leaves for court."

"Oh!" Iris replied. "She does?"

"Northumberland summoned her yesterday." The maid fussed with the table setting. She regarded Iris like a wolf measuring a lamb to see whether it might be swallowed in one bite or two. "The egg girl has come up in the world."

Of course. The maid would wonder why Iris had stayed this night and not the other times, why a kitchen girl from an inn should quarter so near Elizabeth rather than with the servants.

"I . . . was born to a nursery maid here," Iris stammered. "The princess and I played together when we were small. She was very fond of my mother." The girl smiled with one side of her mouth, but not her eyes.

Lies came easier with every one that Iris told. "I shall return to the Red Lion this morning."

"Eat hearty, then." The maid sneered and went away.

Iris sat down at the table alone, staring out at the sky, longing for the bustle she had grown to enjoy in the Lion's kitchen. Even housekeeper Ransom's brusque commands would have been familiar, while here everything was strange.

In the palace gardens, workmen labored already, busy

with clippers at the great topiary bushes. Their outlines sharpened now by the trimming, their shapes were clear: one was a lion and another a stag—no, a unicorn. Iris pushed away a plate of thickly sliced ham and three fried eggs, idly wondering whether these were the very eggs she had brought to the kitchen yesterday.

Her encounter with Northumberland's men seemed a year ago now, but the memory of the man rummaging with his hand in the pocket of her apron still made Iris tremble. She brushed aside the thought. Sweet potatoes from plants that had come from the Indies were mounded on another plate, fried with green chives and shallots. The iridescent sheen on the ham and the sulfurous odor of the eggs made Iris queasy, but she must prepare for travel. She sipped at the mint tea and nibbled at the bread and butter—lovely white bread, with bright strawberry jam. She poured cream into the little pot of porridge and added a spoonful of honey. All the food tasted like straw.

A knock came at the door, and Katherine Ashley entered with a burden of clothing over her arm. She laid the clothes on the bed and pulled the down coverlet over the pillow. The bedclothes were fine red damask worked with gold, but they had been mended time and again. Mrs. Ashley laid out simple linen underclothes—a bodice and petticoat—and a dark green gown with separate sleeves of gold. These were the clothes of another somebody else, to be sure, but a stranger of a different sort altogether. Although the day was already hot, Mrs. Ashley had brought a yellow silk shawl as well.

"We have already packed the other clothing you will need. I have guessed at the size of your feet." Mrs. Ashley eyed Iris's bare feet under the table. "These will do, I think." She set a pair of silken slippers on the floor by the bed and then pulled the corner stool up to the table. "What? Our food is not as good as the Red Lion's?"

"Thank you for the fine breakfast, Mrs. Ashley."

"Kate."

"Kate. I've no appetite."

"And no wonder." Kate buttered the second slice of bread, spread it with jam, and began to eat. "Yesterday the abuse of the duke's man, and today you're a decoy for the hunters."

"Abuse? I was seen?"

"Oh, yes. As the duke has spies, so do we have spies." Kate dabbed at her mouth with a cloth. "Do you remember how Northumberland's man called off the leering varlet who broke the eggs yesterday? The duke thinks that man is his. Though he works for the duke, he's one of ours."

All was deceit and treachery. Iris had been watched by Elizabeth's spies, or Cecil's, who already had reported to Hatfield. What else had she been seen to do? She herself had become deceitful, she whom Lucy and Mother and Father had taught honesty from the cradle. She had been drawn into a web where her life, her self, was no longer her own.

Her life had not been her own, of course, since the day Northumberland took her parents. That she could choose at all was an illusion. In the course of a mere day, she had been orphaned and been reduced to travel among baskets of dusty vegetables. Now—

Kate Ashley interrupted Iris's dark memories. "Set aside your worries, I say. We know about Northumberland's spies in the kitchen; we are using them. Cook shall see to them. A girl will leave for the Red Lion this morning, dressed in your clothes. The spies will see her go."

More deceit. More lies. Iris, whose father had been an earl, had worn the garments of a kitchen maid. Now another liar would wear Iris's false identity, pretending to be the earl's daughter who pretended to be the scullery maid. Meanwhile, Iris the noblewoman would pretend to be a princess. The lies within lies and mysteries within mysteries were too much to comprehend.

She flicked at the ham with the knife.

"Eat, Iris. Who knows when you shall eat such good food again?"

Kate Ashley feared the uncertain future, too. Iris bent to feeding herself. For this morning, another mouthful of porridge with honey and cream. A bite of ham for the noonday. This spoonful of eggs in congealed butter for the supper she might not have tonight, if Northumberland's hunters discovered and seized her. A piece of bread for the morrow. A swallow of ale.

Iris's stomach balked at the thought of more. Mrs. Ashley helped her dress in the green gown, unornamented clothing suitable for a counterfeit princess's journey, then tied the gold silk sleeves in place. They fit Iris as if the seamstress had made them for her.

"'Tis a bit darker than my Elizabeth's," Kate said, drawing back Iris's hair and twisting it at the back of her head, in the style of the princess, "but not so much that men will notice."

The last thing Iris did in her Hatfield room was to transfer her mother's needle and thread from her kitchen maid's skirt to the hem of the green gown.

When she emerged through a door at the back of the palace, near the kitchen, the cobblestone courtyard was crowded and bustling. She drew the shawl up over her mouth. Men loaded a wagon with last-minute baskets—food, perhaps, for common inns were not reliable to satisfy a princess: too much lard and too few fresh peas and greens, if the Lion was typical. Besides, poison was always a hazard.

Restless horses milled about, their hooves clattering on the flagstones, eager to be away, while stablemen held their reins and calmed them with pats on the neck, muttering low words into their velvety nostrils. The great draft horses drawing the royal luggage would have left at dawn, their heavy wagons laden with all that a princess would need at court—if, in fact, a princess had been traveling to court this day. Iris would not have to eat the heavy wagons' dust, and Elizabeth's bed could be assembled at an inn before the company even arrived.

Iris looked up at the windows of the palace. Elizabeth would be watching, grateful for Iris's courage, glad to wish the travelers a safe journey.

The windows were empty. "She cares nothing for us!" Iris blurted to a thickset lady much older than herself, dressed in brown for the dusty journey.

"Hush!" said the woman with quiet intensity, as she tied Iris's shawl. "She slept not a wink for worry, but she mustn't be seen, at the window or anywhere else. Our household spies must not discover that we are but the bait."

Nine men and five ladies of Elizabeth's household held

their own horses' reins. They were decorous and respectful, nodding and bowing a bit whenever Iris drew near them. After her months in the Lion's kitchen, this deference made Iris laugh. Who was she? A countess? A scullion? A messenger? A princess? No. Iris was only a girl, caught up in dangerous times.

One of the men caught her eye, watching her and smiling as she straightened her back like Elizabeth and tossed her head in a haughty attitude. He tipped his chin at her with a sly smile, seeming to read her mind. Combing his dark curls with his fingers, he turned to his horse.

Iris liked the way his doublet fit him, and the muscled legs within his hose. "Who is that gentleman?" she asked a nearby lady.

"He? Oh, he is just Sir Andrew. Handsome fellow, isn't he?"

Iris had expected to be carried in a litter, but a stableman led a white mare toward her, saddled and ready. Iris had not sat a horse of any quality since her departure from Linnetwood, but this mare was finer than any she had ever seen in her life. What joy! She would ride into danger gladly, if she could do it on such a horse. Iris placed her foot in the waiting stableman's clasped hands. He hoisted her up, and she swung her leg over the saddle. The benefit of the green gown's loose cut was clear now; as everyone knew, Princess Elizabeth straddled her horse.

And there beside Iris, astride a black gelding nearly as fine as the white, was Kate Ashley. Kate, of course. Where Princess Elizabeth went, there went Mrs. Ashley, too. Whatever privilege was in the princess's power to confer, Mrs. Ashley received. She maneuvered her horse close to Iris's mare.

"Once past the gate," said Kate, "you must spur your horse—Rose is her name, White Rose—and charge away. The princess waits for no man. You ride well, dear?"

A furtive movement caught Iris's eye. At the end of the courtyard, where an oak tree grew, its gnarled limbs clutching at the sky, a form and a shadow flickered—a girl dressed in a kitchen apron, her hair caught back and tied, the girl who had waited on her at breakfast.

Northumberland's spy.

SEVEN

id Iris ride well, indeed! When she had passed the iron gate in the brick wall and entered the road to London, Iris eased the pressure on the reins and tapped White Rose with her heels. The mare needed urging no more than did Iris. She surged ahead, despite the strangeness of her rider, in rapture at being free to run. Looking back as she passed the men, Iris laughed again. Her shawl floated above her shoulders, its yellow fringes flying. When she looked back, a cloud of dust engulfed the men in her wake. So much for their inky doublets and hose.

Iris rode as if Northumberland himself pursued her, as if to blow off all her grief and anxiety at once and leave it behind in a single joyous flight. She rode as if she would never stop until she had slaughtered Northumberland with her own hand, until she had carried his bloody head over her shoulder through the streets of London. She felt as if Rose had taken wing, faster than a plummeting hawk, faster than—

And then the glorious plunge was over. Rose slowed to a mere gallop, to a trot. Yes, Iris still knew how to ride.

A horseman caught up with her then and seized Rose's bridle. She knew this man and his dark curls, the fellow who had tipped his chin at her.

"Andrew. Sir Andrew Larkin," he said. "A mere knight now, but I shall be an earl someday, when our Princess Elizabeth is queen. I was with you in the courtyard."

"Were you? I didn't notice."

"Oho!" His laughter echoed across the pond that shone beside the road. "She didn't notice!"

Iris laughed, too. She'd not allow this cheeky Sir Curlilocks to flummox her.

"However that may be," said Andrew, suddenly serious, "we are charged with your protection. You cannot ride off like that again."

"I shall do as I like. I am a princess, after all."

He laughed again. "If you do, I shall lead your royal horse, my lady. White Rose and Iris—a nice bouquet. I hadn't known that irises were thorny, too."

He let Rose's bridle go, ticked his heels at his own horse's ribs, and trotted on ahead, just as the entire company drew up around Iris. She turned to trot away after the knight, this Andrew Whoever He Was.

"Stop," said the bronzed and bony Jeremy, who reined in his horse at her side. He spoke softly into her face. "That was a nice chase, but your last. I head this mission. You shall obey my orders, which are these: Stay with the party, at my side. Speak to nobody, show your face to nobody, do nothing without my leave."

"But Mrs. Ashley told me—"

"Mrs. Ashley, at my orders, told you to race away. I now tell you that, for the rest of this day, we shall walk our horses. We shouldn't arrive too soon in London, should we?"

Everything they did would be for show, a deception, a little play for an audience of Northumberland's spies. Even her training in the house of Mrs. Pennefeather had not prepared Iris, the honest girl, for such a life.

"Get off your horse," said the man.

"First tell me your full name."

"Sir Jeremy Boleyn, cousin to Anne."

Elizabeth's kinsman, then, cousin to the princess's mother, Anne Boleyn, whom King Henry had beheaded when he tired of her. Chastened, Iris accepted the help of two men, who had already dismounted to place a small set of steps beside Rose. Iris dismounted, moved away from the horses, and watched. Now Sir Jeremy surveyed the pond, and the ancient oak forest beyond, his right hand on the pommel of his sword. The birds, Iris suddenly realized, had stopped singing, as if they listened. A woodpecker stopped his rat-a-tat and went silent. Perhaps a predator had unsettled them.

"Your horse has gone regrettably lame," Sir Jeremy said. "The race, no doubt."

"No, sir, she is merely catching her breath. This horse could run on to Land's End without a rest."

"Your horse is lame. You see?"

The stablemen had gathered around White Rose. Iris leaned in to watch what they were doing. The farrier, who had followed the noble riders in a cart, held Rose's left foreleg between his leather-covered knees and scraped at the frog of the hoof with a pick. He set the hoof down again. A bald old man knelt and examined the hock. Though no injury was visible, though Iris was certain nothing ill had happened, for the horse had never flagged or stumbled, the man wrapped the mare's hock carefully. Indeed, so carefully did he wrap it that the bandage itself would cause White Rose to limp.

"You see?" said Sir Jeremy at Iris's side. "She's lame. For Northumberland's foxes in the wood. Someone will lead her back to Hatfield, and we shall proceed with greater caution."

"Yes, I see," she said. "Something must slow us down."

The stablemen removed the saddle from Rose, and one of them led her away. They returned with their tools to their small cart at the rear. Iris mounted Sir Jeremy's own black horse, while Boleyn himself took the mount of a man who now rode in a cart. The party went on together more leisurely.

As they approached a farmstead along the way, Sir Jeremy called to the goodwife for water. She hurried to the side of the road, carrying two heavy oaken buckets on a yoke across her shoulders. Six children of varied ages followed her, all silent and agape and round-eyed.

Watchers along the road and in the forest would be aware of Iris's every movement. She must play the part of a princess. No more laughter at her protectors. No more rebellion. The web was woven so tightly that Iris now needed Elizabeth, and Elizabeth depended upon Iris for her life.

"Here, my lady Elizabeth," the farmwife called, hurrying forward with one bucket, the ladle thrust before her. Not a drop splashed out. "Wet your whistle, my princess."

"Whom can I trust? The water might be poisoned," Iris said to Sir Jeremy.

"She's a simple woman. The people love my lady."

With no more hesitation, Iris took the woman's ladle and drank her fill. "Thank you," she said, glancing at the companions on horseback about her. "I shall remember your kindness, as shall we all." Iris turned to her master. "Something for this woman, Sir Jeremy." She could dish up orders, too.

Sir Jeremy bowed his head slightly. "My lady." With a small smile playing at his mouth, he found a gold coin in his doublet, leaned down, and placed it in the woman's hand. The coin would equal her earnings from many years' hard labor. She smiled broadly. Though she was young, not a tooth did she have in her head.

"We'll never forget," the woman said. "Derek—my husband—died a year agone. The sweats. We've seen but little money since."

As they walked their horses away, Curlilocks rode up beside Iris. "Nice work. She didn't turn an eyelash." He smirked. "Don't congratulate yourself too much just yet, however. Were you riding the horses of the moon and accompanied by her starry ladies and gentlemen, folk would mistake you for the moon goddess." He laughed and rode away again.

They passed the Red Lion at mid-morning without stopping to rest, for everyone there knew Iris's face too well. Surely they would recognize her, even if she were riding Lady Moon's horse. They stopped at noonday and sat in the shade of a giant chestnut tree. Kate Ashley introduced the other ladies—Margaret and Lettice, both of them the young daughters of nobles; Harriet, an old lady; and Mallory, the heavy woman in brown who had hushed Iris at Hatfield when she objected to Elizabeth's lack of interest in her.

Together the women opened baskets filled with cheese and wine; cooked sweet potatoes and green onions dressed in vinegar and oil and seasoned with rosemary and thyme; rosemary-flavored bread; cold beef and chicken; plum cake and marmalade. Iris ate despite her small appetite. When she lay back in the grass, so did her attendants.

"Good," said Kate. "The others cannot rest until you do." She arranged a netting over Iris to keep the flies and midges away from her face and hands.

Iris closed her eyes and drowsed, wondering at the sudden turn her life had taken.

⬧⬧⬧

They resumed their slow travel and rode all afternoon. The sun had dropped more than halfway down the sky when Sir

Jeremy held up his hand and stopped the company. "We shall stay the night at the Ladle," he said. He turned to Iris. "I am sorry to say, madam, that you have fallen ill. So ill, indeed, we shall not be able to leave the inn on the morrow." He dismounted and took the reins of Iris's horse. "Down. A princess as sick as you must ride the rest of the way in a cart."

Iris did her best to look weak as Sir Jeremy helped her from her horse down the portable steps. At the wayside she made a fuss, pretending to be sick in the grass. The ladies fluttered around her, as Kate Ashley took charge.

"Here, you—Andrew. Margaret. Quickly." She helped Iris onto a wooden chest, removed from a cart and set in the grass, on which the word "Gowns" was written in a clear, neat hand. Sir Andrew and the lady fitted the wooden boxes, sacks, and baskets in the cart more closely to make a flat surface, and two men replaced the chest alongside. A gold initial "E" decorated banners that flapped in the brisk wind. As Iris waited, her arms clutching her stomach, Lettice unrolled a featherbed and linens and pillows for a pallet on top of the jumble. How this pretense resembled Iris's childhood play with her cousins. Amusing—but she sobered at the thought of the watchers in the woods.

Nearby, Sir Jeremy dispatched a rider to stop the train of horse-drawn wagons that had left Hatfield before dawn. The ladies helped Iris into the cart, where she lay with her back against a knobby sack of sweet potatoes or shoes or something equally hard, recalling her flight in the vegetable cart to William Cecil's house. Mrs. Ashley sat beside her, stroking her hair. Ahead, the road spooled out between the trees. Birds were everywhere, flitting overhead, so many so near, their songs trilling above the squeaks of the horses' leathers and the groans of the cart. Iris turned over on her front to see ahead. In the distance was the sign of the Golden Ladle Inn, a huge dipper pouring stars into a bowl.

Men hastened from the great inn as the royal company entered the courtyard. The innkeeper must have made much business from the princess's many visitors, but it wasn't every day that Elizabeth herself stopped here. Other workers ran from the stables and took the horses' reins from the riders, who clambered down and stretched. The late sun dazzled on the inn's whitewashed walls.

The innkeeper was resplendent in white hose, worn with black knee-length pantaloons and a black jerkin embroidered with scarlet lilies. He hurried to Sir Jeremy, a grin on his florid face. "Welcome, welcome. 'Tis a privilege to entertain my lady Elizabeth." As Iris sat up, he caught her eye. "She's ill? Our princess stops at the Golden Ladle for the first time in her life, and she's ill?" He turned to the door of the inn and roared orders. "Ella! Hannah! Prepare the fine room. Hurry! She's ill."

A serving girl held aside the blowing white curtains, leaned out the casement window above, and called in a lilting, elated voice. "Bring the princess up. We've already changed the linen and puffed the featherbeds. The ale is poured, the water's fresh. Flowers is on the table." Wherever Elizabeth went, people were joyous.

Kate Ashley helped Iris off the cart, her arm around Iris's shoulder in a protective way that also shielded her face somewhat from others' sight.

"Ah, her hair's ablaze, as they say," said a maid in a low voice as Iris passed.

"Beauty," answered another. "And the green frock and golden sleeves—"

"Hush," said the innkeeper, slapping the nearest one. "About your business. Roust the folk from the nearby rooms. Princess Elizabeth's company will take their beds. We shall all sleep in the hayloft."

Two men stood beside a bench where they had been sitting, watching Iris intently. When one of them caught her eye, she stared him down, pulling the yellow shawl higher around her face. He blinked and looked away, but his glance flitted back to her, sly and calculating. Northumberland's man, Iris surmised. She straightened her back and walked into the inn as tall and imperious as she could manage, with Mrs. Ashley still supporting her.

EIGHT

 his great inn was no Red Lion. The Ladle could keep sixty-five people without crowding them. Iris was to stay in the best upper rooms of the inn, a suite with a small sitting room and a separate sleeping room furnished with several small cots. The ladies would sleep here with her, the gentlemen in the nearest of many other rooms.

Servants carried in Princess Elizabeth's own portable bed, of walnut carved with oak leaves and apples and grapes. Fitting wooden tongues into slots, and stabilizing the joints with wooden pins, they assembled the bed in the center of the room.

"I thought the bed went on ahead with the other goods," said Iris.

"The train of stores was not too far ahead," said Mrs. Ashley. "The carters brought a few things back, just as we planned."

Elizabeth's ladies made up the bed with linens from Hatfield that had been pressed with thyme and rosewater, whose scent soon filled the room. They hung scarlet silk curtains from the bedposts and frame. These draperies would protect Iris from the eyes of whatever curious maid might enter the room; the canopy above would catch whatever might fall from the overhead thatch—a mouse, or bird droppings, or bugs.

Iris felt relief. Bedbugs were a traveler's scourge, hiding in the crevices of bed frames and mattresses at every inn along the road. None would sup on her blood tonight.

Two of her attendants—Iris had begun to think possessively of Elizabeth's ladies, as if they were her own—went to cook her supper, making a loud fuss as they left the rooms, for the benefit of listeners.

"She'll eat nothing, with her uneasy belly," said one.

"We shall eat it ourselves, then," said the other, "if she cannot."

Further cause for relief: Iris need not risk poison, should some partisan of the duke have murder in his heart. That safeguard was a good thing, for Iris was ravenous. When Margaret and Lettice returned with the meal, they put it on the table, which Mallory and Harriet had already set with pewter dishes and tankards. They all sat down to eat.

Mrs. Ashley ladled a simple beef stew into a bowl and set it before Iris. Last autumn's carrots and sweet potatoes and new onions floated in the broth, and small green beans and leaves of thyme, fresh from Hatfield's gardens.

"You need not wait on me," said Iris.

Kate went on serving the others. "Oh, but I must. 'Tis not for your sake that I serve you, dear," she said, her shrewd eye on Iris. "We must not treat you familiarly, lest we forget in public for a moment and be seen to do so. Though you are likable enough, you merely stand in for my princess."

Iris put down her spoon. The effect was as if Kate had slapped her. Time and again, Iris had noticed that she had lost her footing, but now that loss had been spoken aloud. Since the day the carter had transported her to William Cecil's house among the vegetables and she stopped being the Earl of Bentham's daughter, her sense of herself had collapsed. She had no sooner met William Cecil than he sent her with Mrs. Pennefeather to be trained as spy and messenger. From then to now, women of small intelligence and culture had ordered her about.

Iris had submerged her very self. She had accepted her role in the kitchen, had even come to like peeling a carrot or boning a leg of lamb. She had enjoyed her growing usefulness. Now she had lost that part as well. She had become a manikin, a mere passive stand-in for the genuine Elizabeth. Neither a scullion nor a princess, the true Iris had quite disappeared.

She had thought these thoughts again and again, but now Kate Ashley had made them audible, for all to hear. Standing suddenly, Iris threw down her napkin, her rage mounting by the instant. She grasped Kate Ashley's wrist in a fury and pulled her to her feet as well. "No, madam. Although I serve the princess, I am no mere stand-in. I am the daughter—only child—heir— of the Earl of Bentham. While a role must be played, the actor who plays the role is herself a nobleman's daughter. You will do well to remember I am noble in my own right."

As she recalled her condition, Iris sank back into her seat, and her voice softened. "Was. *Was* noble, until Northumberland seized my father's title and estate."

Mrs. Ashley curtsied low to Iris. "No. *Are.* So you *are* noble, madam. I beg your pardon. In the end you will reap recompense for your loss and reward for your sacrifice." She observed Iris for a moment. "But, my dear, we mustn't let pride carry us away."

Iris relaxed and gasped a heavy ragged breath as she overcame her attack of grandeur. "I am sorry," she said. "I have shuttled from pillar to post since my parents' deaths. I myself hardly know my name."

Kate Ashley nodded. "Never mind. None of us does. The world has shaken us all once more."

"With the king dead," said the yellow-haired Lettice, her arm encircling Iris's waist, "who knows what will befall Elizabeth, or any of us?"

"Come now." Mrs. Ashley pressed Iris into the bench and sat down at her side again. "Today, we shall eat our supper.

We shall sleep here tonight, and perhaps again tomorrow. Northumberland has gambled that Mary is a fool and a coward. She will disappoint him, I am certain."

"All depends upon Mary, to be sure," said Lettice.

"This day, this hour, we assure Princess Elizabeth's safety," Mrs. Ashley said. "We shall do so until Mary's men capture Northumberland. Tuck in. Eat up. The stew is fine."

Iris bent to her bowl. Starving herself would do no good, and the meat and gravy and vegetables tasted fine indeed. Gentle breezes blew the curtains. Beyond the windows and the plastered white wall, the sun had dropped behind the western trees as always. The world went on.

But now came the sound of scraping chairs and benches from below. Footsteps on the staircase. Jostling and thuds, as if someone had been shoved against a wall.

"Hold," said a loud voice. "Sir Jeremy Boleyn here, master of the Lady Elizabeth's household. What is your business?"

"Lettice," said Mrs. Ashley. "Go to the kitchen for a bowl of water. Iris, you must change into a gown, then into bed with you—Harriet shall help. And Margaret, clear the dishes. Take them down the back stairs."

The men below talked, their voices rising to a half-shout, falling to a mutter, and then rising once again.

"Very well." Sir Jeremy's voice again. "We shall inquire of Mrs. Ashley."

Iris hurried behind the silk draperies, and began, with Harriet's help, to remove her many layers of clothing and prepare herself for bed. Beyond the curtain came a knock, and the door squealed on its hinges.

"Sir Andrew," said Harriet in Iris's ear.

Iris poked her head between the panels of scarlet silk. "I want to hear. This matter concerns me rather closely."

"Indeed." Sir Andrew smiled. "The two gentlemen who observed you so sharply, Princess Elizabeth—"

"That is scorn enough," Iris broke in.

"Yes. I beg your pardon, my lady," said the knight. "No scorn intended. I must call you by the name of the one you play, lest I forget when we are overheard."

"It was scorn," said Iris, feeling more like her old self, now that her dander was up.

"Yes," Sir Andrew stammered. "It was. I do apologize. The two below—they are, of course, Northumberland's men. Hearing you are ill, they've brought a leech."

"We'll have no doings with physicians here," said Kate, "particularly not with Northumberland's yokel sawbones. He would send a healthy woman to the grave."

"Of course," said Sir Andrew. "Sir Jeremy sent me to ask our princess what she wishes done. Does she want the ministrations of the quack?"

"Certainly not," said Kate.

"But if they see me 'ill,'" said Iris, "we might mislead them. They might let down their guard, while we delay. We might gain time."

"Very well," said Mrs. Ashley. "Send them up. But tell them that they must be quiet."

Margaret piled the dishes on a tray and hurried into the sitting room, to leave by an out-of-the-way door. Lettice came in with the bowl of water and set it by Iris's bed, as Mallory closed the window drapes to darken the room. Feeling perfectly well, but fearful, Iris climbed the steps of the high bed and slipped between the linens. When Northumberland's men and the physician entered the suite, she was breathing in short grunting gasps, as Mrs. Ashley bathed her face and neck and hands with a cloth.

"There, there, madam. Your fever is rising, 'tis why you feel so ill," said Kate, "but no rash yet."

More deceit—so much deceit; pretense of illness would soon make Iris sick.

Northumberland's two men backed out through the door into the hallway. The third man, the leech, tied a long parchment beak on his face, with holes cut for his eyes. It was the conical mask many physicians wore to protect themselves from the plague, to keep the fumes of disease at a distance from their faces.

"Oh," Iris groaned, taking the deception further, "may it not be the plague. The king, my darling brother—if I live through this, I shall be too late to say good-bye."

Never to say good-bye, indeed. No good-byes for Elizabeth and King Edward. None for Iris and her parents. Mother and Father, dragged away without a kiss, had been imprisoned and died without the comfort of their child's presence, had died alone, just like Anne Boleyn. In bereavement, at least, Iris and Elizabeth were sisters.

Now Iris needed no deception. The tears that coursed down her face were the real thing. She groaned in genuine agony. She clutched the sheet and held it to her face as the past six months struck her with a towering wave of grief. "The basin," she said. An unfeigned spasm in her belly made her retch.

Lettice held a pewter basin, and Kate held Iris, while she expelled all she had eaten, and more—the grief of the past months; her revulsion for John Dudley, the Duke of Northumberland; her fear of following her father to the scaffold. Nevertheless, she was not so ill that she failed to see the beak of the doctor withdraw as he backed out the door behind his sponsors, to retreat as far and as fast as they could go from the princess with the plague.

NINE

"ris, are you truly ill?" asked Kate Ashley when the men had gone.

"'Tis naught but my old grief. And fear—a little fear."

Iris fell weeping into Mrs. Ashley's arms. When she had wept out all her anxiety and sorrow, she began to laugh. "Did you see how the brave leech quailed when he thought I had the plague?"

The others joined her laughter.

"He couldn't back out fast enough," said Mallory, mocking him in mime.

"'Ooh,'" quavered Harriet, "'let me be gone from this house of contagion.'"

Gradually their fear evaporated in ridicule of their enemies, and Kate stood again. "We have hardly caught our breath after the journey. Let us wash ourselves and sleep. The Ladle's servant girls will wash our linens for us. We shall wash yours, Iris, lest some coward try to kill you with a poison powder. Accept nothing from any hands but ours."

Iris shuddered. "How can Princess Elizabeth sleep at night, knowing her enemies are everywhere? Even in her own household. She is just a girl, like me."

"She has lived the whole of her nineteen years in a cloud of others' malice," said Mrs. Ashley.

"She grew up knowing the Catholics hate her because she's a Protestant," said Lettice.

"Princess Mary hates her because Mary's a Catholic," said Harriet, "and because Anne Boleyn seduced King Henry."

"And Northumberland hates Princess Elizabeth and Princess Mary equally—Queen Mary, now that their brother has died—because he drools after power," said Mallory.

"Enough," said Kate Ashley. "Remember, though half the world may hate Elizabeth, the other half adores her. Friends who would die for her surround her. She sits in a circle of light. We shall find courage again in sleep."

More profoundly than ever, Iris realized she stood under an ax, serving Elizabeth. She was not willing to die for the princess's sake. If Northumberland should capture her, however, he would as likely kill her for being the Earl and Countess of Bentham's daughter as for impersonating Princess Elizabeth.

Iris felt faint with exhaustion. She bathed in the bowl of cool water, enjoying a shiver as it drizzled down the back of her neck and shoulders. As she washed her legs and feet, she picked up the front of the white gown to study the butterfly embroidered there, admiring the expert work.

Mrs. Ashley blushed. "Yes, mended," she said, "but we try to make the patches and repairs beautiful. The king or Northumberland or whoever holds the purse strings has starved us. Were we not frugal and resourceful with what we have, we should all be dressed in rags and eating bark." She reached out her hand to brush the butterfly with tender fingers. "On rainy days, we stitch. This embroidery is her own handiwork. My girl's. Elizabeth's. Though she hates to sew, she does it well, as she does everything."

Iris touched the butterfly with more respect. Everybody knew that the princess could play the virginals and the lute. She could read and write Latin and Greek and spoke several languages, some of them fluently. She knew the history of Europe and the power struggles that troubled relations among England and Spain and France.

Somehow Elizabeth's skill with a needle endeared her to Iris, who found her mother's embroidery needle and floss in the green gown's hem and showed them to Kate and the others. "'Tis all that I have of my mother's things," Iris said.

"She cooks as well, my lady does," said Lettice. "She makes fondant and other sweets every Christmas for the stablemen."

But Mallory gave Iris a clumsy embrace, and Harriet patted her hand.

"There is solace in needlework," said Kate.

Iris replaced the needle in the hem of the green gown. "Are you as tired as I am?" she asked.

The ladies made up all their beds in one room, leaving the second room empty. Iris fell back into the featherbed and pillows, and pulled up the sheet and blankets to cover her ear. She slept as soundly as a bear in its winter den, with Kate at her side and the other ladies on the cots provided by the inn.

By the time dawn broke, the unusually fair weather of recent days had given way to storms. The gunmetal sky hung low, and distant thunder threatened rain. Mist engulfed the westward trees. A light drizzle had skimmed everything with a silver surface, though in the distance a stag and several does browsed on the grassy verges of the ride.

At the window, Iris groaned and stretched away the kinks from the strange bed. When the weather was damp, the knee she had hurt in the cupboard behind the armoire still ached.

"You should try the cots," said Mallory, rubbing her hip bones.

"I'll take a turn this night," said Iris.

"You mustn't," Kate admonished her, shaking her by the shoulders. "You mustn't forget for a moment that you are a princess. Counterfeit, yes, but only we know that. We all must act our parts."

A counterfeit princess, indeed, a pretender to the royal blood she was, yet Iris felt surer of herself this morning than she had felt for months. Breakfast was boiled eggs—these the inn could provide without risk of poison—mint tea and watered ale, and the cheese and porridge the company had brought with them from Hatfield. Lettice lit a fire at the hearth, where Iris warmed her hands and feet and luxuriated in this unaccustomed rest.

"Look." She held up her poor worn hands for the others to see. Her stained and broken nails and the scabby scratches from pecking hens would give her away, should anyone see her hands up close. "Why, they will begin to heal if I keep up this indolence," she told Elizabeth's ladies.

As Iris dressed, she found a jay's feather delicately embroidered in blue and green silk within a crimson wreath on the bosom of her chemise. She looked about her and caught Mallory's eye. The waiting woman smiled slightly and looked away, then came to throw a woolen shawl around Iris's shoulders. Iris caught Mallory's hand and kissed it.

"I put the needle and most of the crimson floss back in their place in the hem of your gown," said Mallory. "I know the needle and thread are precious to you, so I used only two single strands."

Iris nodded, grateful for the gift of the embroidery, grateful for Mallory's acknowledgment, grateful for friendship.

From a trunk, Kate removed several carved walnut cases, opened them, and revealed musical instruments within. "Mallory plays the hautbois," she said, handing the long black woodwind to her. "Margaret plays the flute. And Harriet, like Elizabeth, the lute." Harriet set to tuning the strings, as Mallory soaked the hautbois's reed in a tankard of water.

"But they'll hear below," said Iris.

"Of course they will," Lettice agreed. "They will expect it. The princess never goes anywhere without music."

They played an Italian trio, Harriet taking the part of the virginals on her lute. Iris shivered. Her mother had played the hautbois even better than Mallory. Its reedy, melancholy tone, heard for the first time since Northumberland's men took her parents away, swamped Iris. She went to the window again and looked out over the dripping landscape. The deer had gone to their beds in the woods. Now cows and a few sheep grazed in a pasture between the inn and the forest. Iris longed for the past, when she could wander the fields and forests of her father's estate, in rain or shine, on horseback or on foot, with companions or alone, whatever she chose. She passed her open hand across her face, as if to wipe away her history with her tears and to enjoy this lovely moment of music for its own sake.

"I once could play the virginals myself," she said quietly. "Mother taught me how."

Mrs. Ashley kissed the nape of her neck.

Hearing hoofbeats, many horses, on the road, Iris stepped back from the casement window to see without being seen. The horsemen in such a hurry wore Northumberland's green livery. One group of several men, headed for London, pulled up their horses beside another group, headed in the opposite direction. The men who had come from court gestured, pointing north, then sweeping their hands toward the south.

Both groups wheeled their horses toward the Ladle, galloped into the courtyard, tied their mounts to the rail, and stood talking in the dooryard of the inn. Iris put her finger to her lips. The hautbois and flute went silent. Although the men's voices were indistinguishable from one another, an occasional word and phrase floated up, whole and clear: "Mary." "Escaped to the east." "Mary." "Mary's army." "Catholics." "Men gathering from the countryside."

One of them lifted his horse's hind hoof between his knees and inspected it. He ran his fingers up the leg. Then, the bridle in his hand, he led the horse around the corner of the inn toward the stable.

"What is it, Charles?" called the apparent leader of the troop.

The horseman returned to the end of the building. "Only a scratch on his hock. I shall have the stable boy smear it with turpentine salve."

"Don't keep us waiting."

"Not at all."

Sir Jeremy and Sir Andrew came out of the inn. "What news? How is the king's health?" called Sir Jeremy. They joined the others in the dooryard, clapping them on the back and shaking hands. The men chatted, raked their hands through their hair and scratched their beards, like ordinary men meeting at a street corner. From her place near the window, Iris would have sworn they all were friends and associates, all working for a common cause, not two groups of partisans playing a murderous game of chess with living pieces.

And Iris was a pawn.

TEN

After Northumberland's men had gone, Sir Jeremy and Sir Andrew came to report what they had learned.

"Let us be sure we are alone," said Sir Andrew. He opened the door to the sitting room, exclaimed, and bounded through. Sir Jeremy rushed to help. A moment of scuffle and clatter and shouts and thuds followed. Through the open door, Iris glimpsed one of the men who had gazed at her so intently when the company arrived at the inn. Now, beaten by Elizabeth's two men, he sat leaning against the wall, his legs splayed, his nose bleeding, and his eye already swelling shut. Andrew rubbed his shoulder gingerly. Sir Jeremy's knuckles bled.

"King Edward shall hear of this impertinence," Sir Jeremy growled as he pulled the man to his feet and hustled him out the door at the far end of the room. "Eavesdropping on the king's sister, indeed."

Iris and Mrs. Ashley caught each other's eye.

"Do you suppose he heard?" Iris asked her. "'Counterfeit princess,' you said."

"We spoke but quietly," said Margaret. "And the door was closed."

Kate raised her eyebrows at Iris. "Now you see why we must pretend, even in private."

Nevertheless, dread sat upon Iris's heart, and the ladies fell silent.

The gentlemen returned with a heavy key, with which Sir Jeremy locked the outer door of the empty room. "Nobody will spy there again, unless he be the innkeeper, with a second key in hand. What might the man have heard?"

"Nothing of consequence," said Mrs. Ashley.

Sir Jeremy sat down at the bench and leaned his arms on the table. He poured a tankard of ale from the ewer he had brought. "They've no idea we know King Edward has died," he said. "They believe we are headed for London."

"How can you be sure?" asked Kate. She held out her own tankard while Sir Jeremy poured.

"One of the riders from London. It seems we have as many partisans in Northumberland's service as he has himself. The fellow spoke to our Nicholas in the stable."

The rider who had said his horse's leg was hurt: he was the princess's man.

"Nor do they realize we know of Guildford and Lady Jane's marriage and Northumberland's plot. Lady Jane was unwilling, our gentleman said, but her father beat her into submission, poor lass. She fainted when Northumberland proclaimed her queen. The council showed her a document with King Edward's signature, ordering that his sisters' right to the throne be bypassed."

"Poor lad, he didn't know what he was signing, I'll warrant!" sputtered Mrs. Ashley.

"Ill as he was, the king would have signed anything Northumberland gave him," said Sir Andrew.

"Better a Protestant Queen Jane, they would have told King Edward," said Mrs. Ashley, "than a Catholic Queen Mary. As if Northumberland had any religious scruple—he merely wants to save his skin. What gall. Jane is so devout in her religion, she would believe them, too."

Sir Jeremy gripped the tankard with both of his hands. "Elizabeth's trouble deepens by the day." He nodded at Iris. "They still think you are she, but they grow impatient. Why is she not continuing to London? they want to know. How serious is her illness? A doctor who knows Elizabeth is riding here from London."

"He will recognize me as the imposter I am," said Iris. "I shan't be caught here like a mouse smoked in its hole."

Iris threw a silken slipper across the room, the temper Mother and Lucy had tried so hard to quench running away with her. She was afraid—but more than fear, she resented Sir Jeremy's control of her fate. She was full to bursting of being moved about at others' whim, used to block the movement of a knight here and a rook there, an easy sacrifice for defense of the king and queen. Elizabeth's servants had protected Iris until now, but they had also led her into harm's way in the first place, else she should need no protection.

"When they discover me, they will have Elizabeth as well, within a few hours," Iris said.

"True," said Sir Jeremy. "We may none of us escape alive."

Iris's impatience boiled over. "I shall not sit still to be taken! My home is but twenty miles from this place. I know the country thereabouts, near Linnetwood, my father's house, as once I knew the geography of my own bedroom. Nobody yet knows, either, that I am not Elizabeth or who I am, in fact."

"We cannot escape," said Sir Jeremy. "We cannot travel fast enough. We cannot disguise such a large troop."

"Who said aught of 'we'?" Iris said. "'Can't never did anything,' my Lucy used to say. I shall take one other person. A woman. We shall sleep in farmers' byres or the forest."

Sir Jeremy stood abruptly, clattering the bench, a storm brewing on his face. "You rise above your station, my girl."

Iris faced him, her spirit now loosed. She would not tuck it away again—not for Sir Jeremy, not for Princess Elizabeth, not for anyone. "I remind you, sir, I am your superior in rank. Now listen well. When the court physician arrives, delay him as long as he allows. When he discovers I am gone, the duke's men will pursue me, still not knowing that the princess remains at Hatfield."

"Go on."

Iris's heart pounded. Her bravado rang ridiculous in her own ears, yet she persisted. "I shan't let them catch me. My escape will afford you more time to move Elizabeth to safe quarters and gather an army around her. Northumberland's men will think she has eluded the snare. While they chase me, the wild goose, she may get away, in fact."

The men scowled at one another.

"Off your high horse, my girl. The plan is too risky," said Sir Jeremy, "and we have already sent a courier to Hatfield. You are not a princess. You only play at being one."

"As you say. But neither am I an egg girl, or merely a messenger for William Cecil. Lest you forget, Sir Jeremy, I am the Earl of Bentham's daughter. I am my father's daughter in spirit as well as rank. You will have to bind and gag me—kill me, indeed—to hold me here, a docile mouse trembling behind the wainscot, awaiting the cat's claws."

"I shall go with you," said Sir Andrew.

"No. You must stay here," Iris said. "For as long as we can deceive them, they must not suspect the bird has flown."

Sir Jeremy considered. "As you propose," he said at last. "Mallory rides nearly as well as you. She shall go with you. Do not be caught, my girl. You have made fools of them. They would kill you on the spot for that offense alone."

Thinking of the embroidered feather, Iris turned to Mallory. The lady consented with a nod. Iris reached for her hand and kissed it.

"Dressed in common clothes, two females will be invisible." Sir Jeremy stared into space and thought. He paced the floor. He looked out the window at the misty forest. He hummed and cleared his throat, then drummed his fingers on the door frame. "You will take two horses sturdy enough to be reliable, but not so fine as to attract attention." He turned to Mallory. "You are willing to accompany this madwoman?"

"I am."

"Then go at midnight with my blessing. Mallory, your experience is the greater. You shall command this girl. Iris, you shall obey."

Obey? Ha! Iris had had enough of obedience.

She and Mallory ate as much as they could, not knowing when they would eat another full meal. They waited impatiently for the sun, which set late now, the height of summer. At last, when deep dark had fallen, they went out the back door dressed in the women's clothes that Lettice had pinched from the inn's laundry; some poor serving maids would have to do without their second dresses and aprons.

Iris handed a parcel to Lettice. "After our scheme is discovered, please give these gowns to the servants whose clothing you took. The gold lace alone will support them for a year."

Disguises in place, and trying not to be noticed, Iris and

Mallory crossed the torchlit stableyard, talking and forcing soft laughter. Even now, as the time neared midnight, and despite the danger of highwaymen, the place was busy with travelers coming and going. A great burst of laughter blew from the windows of the inn's serving rooms, where men stayed up to drink and talk and lose money wagering on dice. Nobody paid the least attention to the two women walking across the yard.

Saddled horses awaited them in the shadows, already laden with bundles of food, blanket rolls, and two oiled canvas sheets to protect them from rain and damp. They walked their horses along the road until they were well out of earshot of the inn, then urged them to a trot, and then a gallop. Down the road a way, when they stopped to listen, the distant clops of other horses drifted to them.

"We are followed," said Mallory.

"Good," Iris replied. "At least we know where the watchers are. They saw us leave, but they are uncertain who we are."

No moon or starlight lit the road, and the overcast sky and heavy air promised rain. They traveled on at a moderate but steady pace. After they passed a sharp elbow in the public road, Iris swerved her horse into the roadside ditch, signaling Mallory to follow her.

"No!" Mallory stopped her horse in the middle of the roadway. "Sir Jeremy ordered me to take you by the most direct route."

"Sir Jeremy did not know we would be followed, and you take me nowhere, Mallory. Wherever I go now, I take myself."

Iris's new resolve propped her up. No longer a pawn, she was a player now, moving chessmen of her own.

Mallory hesitated.

"Hurry!" said Iris. "Either go on alone, or come with me. Our minders will be upon us in a moment." She whirled her horse and spurred him in among the thick undergrowth at the edge of the wood.

Mallory followed. Within the protection of the trees, they pulled up their horses and stopped to watch the road. Moments later the pursuing horsemen passed, riding fast.

When sound of their horses had ceased and no others came behind them, Mallory reached for Iris's reins. Iris spurred her mount away.

"You are in my charge, Iris. I shall make the decisions here. Sir Jeremy—"

"No. I shall do my best for the princess, but I shall save myself," Iris said. "You may come with me or no, as you see fit, but decisions concerning me are mine alone."

Mallory stammered, then fell silent as Iris sat her horse and waited, watching the road.

"Now where?" asked Mallory at last. "We can't just take the road behind them."

"Hush. Listen. Wait a bit."

Soon came the sound of two more horses, followed a moment later by the horses and riders themselves.

Mallory let out her breath. "Those two would have captured us, had we returned to the road."

"Trust nothing in such times as these," Iris said. "Now into the wood. Northumberland's men will think we two have vanished into the night air."

"Until they remember where they saw us last."

"They will not remember precisely where," said Iris. She laughed. "We'll spend this night here in the wood. They'll never guess we've stopped within a whistle of the Ladle."

Iris let her horse pick its own way into the darkness among the trees, keeping her face low on its neck to protect her eyes from branches, and Mallory's mount followed. The forest was as dark as the inside of a closed mouth, as dark as the cupboard where Iris had hidden the day Northumberland's men arrested her parents, yet the horses slowly found a way between the trees. Soon, beyond the brush that grew in the roadside sun, the oaks were ancient, with huge trunks, and branches so thick that the forest floor was clean.

Iris and Mallory rode until they came to a brook, where their horses stopped to drink at its gravelly edge. There they dismounted, wiped the horses dry of sweat, and settled the animals close together on the ground in a drift of old oak leaves they quickly gathered. They tied a canvas shelter to branches overhead, for a light rain had begun to fall again. Huddled between the horses, taking advantage of their warmth, the women covered both the animals and themselves with blankets; even in July, a rainy night was cold, and if the rain should stop, the midges would drive them all mad unless they protected themselves.

"What shall we name them—the horses?" said Mallory.

"Mine is already named. Courage."

"Then mine shall be Hope," Mallory said.

Courage sighed. Soon Mallory began to snore softly. Iris was glad to rest, yet she could not sleep. She leaned against her own mount's back, savoring his gamy scent. Back at Linnetwood, in Thorpe's well-ordered stables, her father had directed the blacksmith and the stable boys, the farrier, the carpenter, and all the other workmen to let her watch, despite her gender, and learn what they knew.

Thorpe and Lucy had slept in rooms near the horses. There they often fed Iris supper and told her stories of the days when they and her father were young, and Iris was a little girl. Elizabeth's father, King Henry, was alive then, and sometimes visited Linnetwood to hunt. The king brought with him a household of fifty men; once two hundred came. They slept in tents on the lawn when Linnetwood's dozens of rooms were filled. While the noblemen roistered and jousted on the lawn, Lucy had fed Iris fine beef stew, and soda bread, hot from the oven, with sweet butter melted into all the pores, and fried cakes, cooked in bubbling lard. When Iris was full, and time for bed had come, Lucy sent a linen-covered basket full of the sweet oily cakes up to the house with her. Once, in the early morning, Iris had caught a glimpse of the fat king in his nightshirt.

As one memory after another rolled across Iris's mind, she grew drowsy. She dreamed she was a child, sharing the settle with Lucy at the stable rooms' hearth, Lucy stroking her hair and humming "The Fox Went Out on a Windy Night." Now she was going home. Lucy and Thorpe would take her in. She would be no more a spy, a scullion, or a counterfeit princess. She would be herself again, and all would be well.

Ever so slowly, secure once more in the remembered embrace of home, Iris slid down into sleep. Tomorrow would be soon enough to plan her return to Linnetwood.

ELEVEN

ris yawned and rubbed away her pains from sleeping on the ground. Having awakened with the sun, Mallory had already laid out a cold meal. The hobbled horses stood now, browsing the grasses that grew thick beside the brook.

"This is an easy morning," said Mallory. "We wake already dressed. No chamber pots to empty. No food to fetch. No dishes to carry away. No fire to stoke. The horses eat what they may find."

Iris gazed through the leaves at the patches of blue sky and fluffy clouds overhead. "Fair weather for a journey, too."

They washed their faces and hands, shivering as they stood barefoot in the cold water of the brook. When they had dried themselves and put on shoes over clean stockings, Iris pulled away the blue-and-white patterned cloth that covered the food. They savored a breakfast of cold beef and boiled eggs and brown bread and shared a corked jug of ale.

"Our next meal will be with farm folk," said Iris.

"Sir Jeremy gave me a purse for the journey," said Mallory. She put her hand inside her clothes and brought out from her bosom the deerskin bag of coins that hung from a cord around her neck.

The power of money was the power to control. Sir Jeremy had treated Iris like a child. Rage rose up, and Iris did not try to damp it down. She held out her hand.

"Sir Jeremy entrusted it to me," said Mallory.

"I will not be subservient." Iris waited, hand still outstretched.

"Oh, Iris, surely by now you have come to your senses. You are but a girl. I am fifteen years your senior."

Still Iris waited. And waited.

Mallory stood up. Turning her back to Iris, she took off the pouch, dropped it into the oak leaves with a chink, and walked away to busy herself with the horses, leaving Iris to repack the food.

Iris had won the test of wills, but she hung the leather bag around her own neck with little satisfaction in the triumph. After all she had been through, she intended never again to be under another person's thumb, but she felt ill at ease, now that she was in charge. Soon she would be back at Linnetwood, though, where Thorpe and Lucy would know what to do.

By noon, Iris had found a track leading north through the woods. She stopped beside a spring and filled the empty ale jug with fresh water. Mallory had said nothing all morning. By suppertime, they had stopped at a cottage, where a woodcutter and his wife fed them, accepting them as travelers in need.

"What do you hear from court?" asked Iris.

"Same as what I hear from the moon," the man said, rubbing his swollen knuckles. "You'ns is the first I see along this track in many a day."

Paid well for her hospitality, the woman packed cheese and bread and cider for the journey. Her husband directed Mallory and Iris to a broader road not far away that would take them on north toward Linnet-upon-Byrne, the village nearest to home. They continued on paths and lanes instead, for fear of Northumberland's watchers on the road. When darkness fell, they had already ridden down through the ditch and into the forest again and settled themselves among trees, great chestnuts this time. The night was cloudy but warm.

Still Mallory had said not a word to Iris and only enough to the woodcutter to be polite. So be it. After tomorrow, Iris would never leave Thorpe and Lucy again. Soon she would need Mallory no more. But even as Iris longed for home, even as she determined to hide herself away in the countryside, she thought of her promise to her dead parents that she would avenge them. And what of Elizabeth? Had Iris succeeded in drawing the hounds away from Hatfield? She laughed softly at the rage they would feel when they discovered her gone and assumed they had lost Princess Elizabeth. Her satisfaction in Northumberland's likely fury softened the hard ground under her back. Nevertheless, as Iris fell asleep, she dreamed again that she was home, with Lucy holding her against her soft bosom and rocking her.

The following day at mid-afternoon, Iris and Mallory arrived in country familiar to Iris. "Lord Rollins's fields," she said, waving her arm at the barley, its color changing from green to silver to green again, as it shifted its weight in the breeze.

"Lord Rollins's fields they must be, if you say so," said Mallory in a haughty tone.

Well, at least she was talking now, angry though she remained, and Iris would not be goaded to answer with anger of her own. The two rode on in silence, passing a herd of cows that grazed in a meadow. Soon they came to the great Monastery of St. Albert. Iris pointed at the burned-out stone hulk.

"See what the Protestants did here," said Iris, pointing as they rode past. "When I was a child and saw these empty windows, I thought the monastery's eyes had been put out. Father said they once contained the most glorious stained glass in all of England."

After a few minutes Mallory spoke again in a thoughtful

voice. "If Mary comes to the throne, perhaps she will take revenge on the Protestants."

Queen Mary. Catholic Queen Mary.

Iris shuddered, remembering all she had heard of old King Henry—his seizure of the monasteries and other Roman Catholic lands; the Catholics executed; the mother of Cardinal Pole, Mary's friend, beheaded. If Mary took revenge, the future would be bloody.

Iris and Mallory passed St. Agnes's, the old Catholic church that King Henry's religious edicts had made a Protestant chapel.

"We used to worship there," said Iris, full of longing.

Religious turmoil had affected far more than King Henry's private life. The sheep grazing in the verdant meadows as far as Iris could see from here fed on lands that once were the property of the Catholic Church. Henry had seized those properties and given them to his Protestant noblemen, in order to seal their loyalty.

Linnetwood itself had been enlarged with Catholic lands. Iris's father and mother and Iris herself had been the beneficiaries of the king's acts against the Church, long before King Henry's son, the Protestant Edward, came to power. Long before Northumberland had taken control of the boy king and had killed his opponents—the Earl of Bentham, for one.

"What do you think, Mallory? Will Mary take revenge?" Iris asked.

"How should I know?" Mallory asked, giving Iris an acid look. "I am but your servant."

Iris took in a sharp breath. Her mother's and Lucy's judgment of her was accurate. She was rebellious. She was a spit-fire, too, as Cecil had heard, her anger erupting easily, though soon giving way to peace. Her high spirits had saved her, and Mallory too. Nevertheless, her treatment of Mallory troubled Iris's kind heart. "Forgive me. I am sorry I wounded you."

They rode on another mile in silence, and then Iris tried again to cross the gulf of anger. "Truly, Mallory, you have been privy to court gossip. Mary—do you think she will take revenge?"

"God knows. Not I." Mallory sighed. "Did you know that Northumberland offered the throne to Elizabeth?"

"Why did she not accept? As a Protestant, she would have spared England great bloodshed."

"Accept the crown from that asp? My lady is too clever for him. Should he win the struggle with Mary, and should Elizabeth be crowned, Northumberland would control her ever after. Should Mary rise against him then, and win, she would execute him and Elizabeth without blinking."

The seesaw of power, Iris mused, might well bring Mary to the throne. An enemy of another stripe, a bitter Catholic. As a Protestant herself, Iris might need the protection of Princess Elizabeth then.

When at last they came to the hamlet of Linnet-upon-Byrne, Iris's excitement interrupted her fretting.

"Now I must hide myself for another reason," Iris said, adjusting the cap on her head and raising the collar of her homespun green jerkin. "Here I might be recognized as myself. What a novelty! To be known as oneself."

"Wait a moment," said Mallory. She leaned from her saddle to tuck a strand of Iris's red hair under her cap.

They clopped across the little bridge that crossed the Byrne, the stream that meandered through the Bentham estate. Here were the very waters where Iris had played as minnows tickled her legs, building dams, wading in shallow water, learning to swim and fish beside her mother and father. Iris and Mallory slowed for a boy and his half-dozen goats, their udders swinging, full of milk for tomorrow's cheese. The two riders picked their way among the chickens that bathed in the dust of the road. Lord Rollins's cowherd, old Tom, moved among the russet-spotted white cattle, perhaps assessing their health, in a pasture near the road, but Iris restrained her impulse to wave and call out to him. Blessed Tom.

"Linnetwood is just around the next bend in the road," said Iris.

"Yes. Now I see the smoke above the trees."

"There's a baker's shop at the crossroads. Ride on ahead and buy us a sack of buns." Iris took the leather bag of coins from her neck and handed it to Mallory, the two exchanging looks that bespoke apology and gratitude. "I mustn't show myself—the baker would know me anywhere, servant's gown or no. I shall wait here and catch up when I see you come out of the shop."

Mallory took with her one of the linen bags that had contained the food from the Ladle. When she had finished her errand, Iris rode to her side. Mallory held out the leather pouch.

"Thank you," Iris said. "You keep it. As you reminded me, you are fifteen years my senior." Power could be shared, as Lucy and Thorpe had taught her, making peace when children quarreled or workers disagreed.

Mallory smiled. "The baker asked where I was headed, of course," she said. "Strangers in this hamlet must surprise her. I told her we were Thorpe's nieces, come for a visit."

Mallory paused, watching Iris sharply. "I should find things much changed, the baker said, if I had visited Linnetwood before. When I asked for more news, she busied herself counting out the buns and wouldn't answer. I felt as if I had only imagined she spoke."

Munching the buns, Iris and Mallory left behind the thatched bakery, where smoke from the chimney climbed the sky and mixed with the scent of something sweet and hot in the oven. Past the village's stone smithy and carpentry shop they went, where the clang of hammer and the rasp of saw rang and whined. Women swept the steps and dooryards at the several cottages of Linnet, calling over fences and staring open-mouthed at the pair of travelers. Near Lord Rollins's gate, a crowd of several children played. "Ring around the rosie," they sang, "a pocket full of posies. Ashes, ashes, we all fall down." Children everywhere knew the song about the plague, its splotchy red rash, and its many dead.

With Linnet behind them, Iris dug her heels into her horse's ribs. "Not far now," she called back to Mallory. Feeling her eagerness, the horses surged ahead.

Mallory caught up and took the reins of Courage. "You're

eager, Iris, as who would not be? But do you know the state of things at Linnetwood?"

Iris stared at her older friend's dark eyes and scowl.

"Things have changed, Iris. Didn't you hear me tell you? We must be careful. Make a plan. Not rush."

Iris gasped as if she had been holding her breath. What a fool! She had been hurrying back to her father's house. To her mother's sewing room and embroidery frame. To Thorpe's and Lucy's settle by the fire. She had willfully turned away from reality.

The knowledge of what she had lost surged through her again. "Thank you, Mallory. You have helped me regain my reason. Of course. We must learn what use Northumberland has made of my inheritance before we blunder into trouble we cannot escape."

They rode along more slowly now, having entered the lands of Linnetwood, following the Byrne through the crowded trees, Iris leading, headed toward Linnetwood's great gate. Nothing had changed that she could detect. The same oak woods grew close to the road, with the stand of old beeches in the distance. The same linnets and robins called. The same sun shone overhead. Everything was as it had always been, always and forever, back through time immemorial, before Iris was born, before her great-great-great-grandfather, whose portrait hung in the gallery.

As they approached the long drive, however, where stone pillars supported an iron gate, Iris reined in Courage. "Northumberland's! The scoundrel!" she shouted. Instead of the Bentham coat of arms, a red bear and a wolf on black, the shields that hung on the pillars depicted Northumberland's green lion and bear rampant on a ragged staff against a ground of yellow. For that, to hang his coat of arms on the Earl of Bentham's gate and gain control of his lands, Northumberland had executed Iris's father.

She tipped her head back and opened her mouth. What poured out was a long cry of anguish.

Mallory lunged for Iris's reins and caught them in her hand. "Hush, Iris!"

But Iris the spitfire was in the saddle again. When she had sworn all the nasty words she ever had heard in the stable and at the Lion, she felt better. "I knew, of course, but did not understand—did not *feel* what I knew," she said, calm at last. "I can but wonder at my own foolishness. Still, Mallory, my old Thorpe will know what to do."

Afternoon had come with such heat that the birds had ceased singing. Only the bees appeared to work. Iris and Mallory tied Courage and Hope beside a forest spring, at a distance from the manor house, so their whinnies would not reveal their presence. Then Iris led Mallory to a vantage point at the edge of the woodland, where they could see the house and grounds, especially the stables and the mullioned windows at the western end of the hewn-stone building—Thorpe's and Lucy's rooms. Iris had watched thus at Hatfield Royal Palace but a few days ago. Now, as then, all seemed peaceful. All but Iris's heart, for this time the house she spied on was her own.

As it had six months ago, the oak tree stood at the corner of the house; Iris fancied she could see the ropes of her childhood swing hanging there yet. The stone house itself glowed golden. Her mother's knot garden still grew at the front of the house, though the rosemary hedges were overgrown. There stood the rose arbor, where Iris had given and received her first kiss—the boy was Adam, son of her father's best friend. Within the week, Mother and Father had been seized, and Iris spirited away in the night and taken to William Cecil's house in London.

Men and women came and went, in and out of the kitchen and the stables, the byre and the styes and the fowl sheds. "There goes Ned," said Iris, "our carpenter. Mary and Catherine, the dairymaids." By the door at the end of the stables stood the bench, just as it always had, where Thorpe smoked his pipe in the evening and watched the westering sun, where Iris had often sat with him, learning to whittle or to tie useful knots. The place was busy as ever. Iris watched in a trance, not grieving now, but bewildered and numb. When darkness fell, she would creep down into the yard and knock at the door. Lucy would take her in, would greet Mallory as kin since she was Iris's friend, would feed them and make them a bed and kiss them good night. Lucy and Thorpe would make things good again, as good as they ever could be with Mother and Father gone.

"What if Northumberland has banished your people—the Thorpes, did you say? What if he has given their places to others? What shall we do?" Mallory asked in a soft voice.

The question startled Iris. "Why should he have done so?

Thorpe is the best stable master in the county. And who could replace Lucy?"

"Just a bit ago, you called yourself foolish."

Iris put her hand to her mouth, stricken by Mallory's good sense. "You are right," she said. "Indeed, what shall we do?"

When the sun had set and darkness had fallen, no candlelight brightened the windows at the end of the stables. Nobody sat on the bench, drawing on a pipe whose embers brightened with every puff. Nevertheless, Iris and Mallory walked down into the workyard. The dog that ran to meet them bellowed a warning, then caught their scent and nearly knocked Iris down in his greeting. It was MacTavish, the curly-haired black-and-white dog she had known from the day he was born. He pranced about them, running in for a nuzzle, circling them at a gallop, his lips drawn back in a grin, all but climbing Iris's body to kiss her in his joy.

If Mac was still here, what could be amiss?

TWELVE

Led by Mac, Iris stole into the stables she knew so well. Mallory held the hem of Iris's jerkin so as not to lose her way, the darkness was so deep. Most of the livestock slept in the meadows now, through the warm July nights; only the sick horses, or other animals that required Thorpe's expert attention, would be in the stalls. A shielded heavy candle burned in the end stall, where a large and restless beast bumped against the wall of planks and the wooden gate. Its size and the noise of great teeth grinding oats told Iris that the animal was a horse.

She tiptoed to the stall, trailing Mallory behind her. The horse was Shadow, his right rear leg bandaged. Her own childhood horse nuzzled her neck. As she petted his velvety nose, something in the dim corner of the stall drew her eye. There lay Thorpe, asleep in a pile of straw, snoring, his mouth agape. He embraced a jug that was upside-down, its contents emptied into either the straw or Thorpe's belly. Even in the dim candlelight, his dishevelment stunned Iris. Several days' growth of white whiskers frosted the jaw and cheeks that always before had been clean-shaven. His tunic was stained. This man could not be Thorpe—their resemblance must be an illusion. Iris drew closer. His face, turned to one side, lay in vomit that had soaked down into the straw.

Lucy never would have stood for such degradation in anyone, least of all in Thorpe. Lucy. Where was Lucy?

Mac waited at the door of the stall, hesitant, as if afraid of Thorpe, the man who had raised and hand-fed the dog from his own plate. Mac followed as Iris took Mallory's hand, led her out of the stables, back along the stone wall, and onto the stoop of Thorpe's and Lucy's rooms. As the door opened, the dog barged through, the head of the household preceding his guests. Iris felt for the tapers that still stood upright in the stoneware crock by the door, but no embers burned on the hearth after the evening meal, no fire lit the room with its glow or provided Iris with a spark for the candle. Lucy must be visiting a neighbor. She always had been a good nurse.

"Lucy," Iris whispered. No answer came. "Lucy," Iris said aloud.

She felt her way to the table at the edge of the room that Lucy had always kept so well ordered. Dirty dishes covered the table's timeworn boards. Iris put a mug to her nose and drew in the sharp scent of spirits stronger than ale or wine. She felt her way to the tidy sleeping room, to Lucy's and Thorpe's bed. Sweet linen covered the wool-stuffed mattress, made up neatly, as if Lucy had just spread freshly washed sheets and tucked them in.

"We'll sleep here," said Iris, "and wait for Thorpe to recover himself in the morning."

"We'll be caught," said Mallory.

"None of the servants would dare to enter Thorpe's rooms."

"But our horses."

"They'll drink from the spring where we tied them. They'll eat the grass."

"Iris, staying here is uncertain—it isn't wise. We can return tomorrow night."

"Do as you wish. I cannot leave until I know what has happened. By the looks of things here"—Iris gestured at the mess around them—"he'll be drunk again by nightfall tomorrow. Lucy—"

The name caught in her throat.

In the morning, the roosters woke Iris and Mallory at the same time, as the sky began to lighten. Mac had slept the night at the foot of the bed. They let him out, found the tinderbox to make a fire at the hearth, and picked up dirty clothing as water came to a boil in the kettles. At least fresh water filled the small oak cask that stood inside the door. Iris washed the dishes, while Mallory dried them and put them away on their shelf. They let Mac back in, then scrubbed the filthy clothing, all of it Thorpe's. Every garment stank. Both of Lucy's coarse linen dresses and her aprons were clean and neatly folded on another shelf, in the sleeping room, opposite the bed. They hung Thorpe's laundered stockings and tunics and pantaloons on the drying rack in the kitchen.

Just as Iris raised the drying rack on the pulley to the ceiling, heavy footsteps sounded at the stoop. Mallory darted into the sleeping room, but Iris turned to the door and waited. The door swung open, and there stood Thorpe.

For a moment, neither he nor Iris moved. Then, both at once, they threw open their arms, rushed across the room, and embraced. They stood apart then, filling their eyes with each other.

"You're grown tall," said Thorpe at last.

"Yes."

"You're safe here, then. Them from the days before your father—" His voice broke. "Them from the old days'll protect you. The new ones'd never know you, even if they could imagine you'd come back." He looked down at himself, at his dirty hands and the food and spots of grease on his tunic, at the straw caught in the creases of his clothes, and folded his arms to cover the stains.

Mac, regaining his trust in Thorpe, nuzzled his hand.

"Never mind, Thorpe." Iris waited. He was no longer the carefree friend of her childhood. She was no longer the child who had sat by his side and watched the sun set as she listened to his stories of the wolves and bears that had roamed the forest when he was a boy. He would tell her in his own time how things stood.

"I brought a friend."

Mallory came out from the sleeping room.

"My friend Mallory," said Iris, with a small curtsy. "My friend Thorpe," she said, with a little bow to him.

"I'll get us summat to eat." Thorpe rushed out, combing his hair with one hand and brushing the backside of his tunic with the other.

Mallory looked around the bright room. "Clean again," she said. "They lived well once, your Thorpe and Lucy."

"They were my father's favorites. Lucy nursed him when he was a babe. Thorpe dandled him on his knee, just as he did me."

Thorpe returned eventually, balancing cheese and a jug of milk and a loaf of bread. He gestured at his clothing, which was clean but damp. "Matthews borrowed me out his extras," he said. "Had me a wash in the horse trough, too. Since Lucy took sick . . ." Thorpe cleared his throat. "She never got over your father's—" He held his forehead in his hand. "John Dudley, King Northumberland himself, strutting about here, damned cock o' the walk."

Father. Mother. Now Lucy as well. More of Iris's own heart's blood on Northumberland's hands.

"Lucy? Let me see her, Thorpe."

"Not until you eat. Pains in her chest attacked her a fortnight ago. She grows sicker by the day—I blame the cur Northumberland." He poured milk into mugs and cut bread and cheese into thick slabs. Then he turned away to wipe his eyes and nose. "Robinson is seeing to her—you remember, Cook's helper. Eat, my girl. Then I'll take you to her."

Iris slid beside Mallory onto a bench by the table and ate as if it were her duty, now and then slipping morsels to Mac, who sat and waited for this reward. Thorpe took only the heel of the dark bread and sips of milk. He watched Iris as if he feared she might evaporate if he blinked.

"After Cecil's man took you off in the wagon, we never heard more," he said. "Alive or dead, none of us knew. Lucy couldn't bear it."

As the three of them ate breakfast, Iris told Thorpe about her training as Cecil's messenger and spy; her labor as egg girl and scullion at the Red Lion; her errands to Hatfield Royal Palace. She told him of the ruse Princess Elizabeth had devised, and of her own part in it, while Mallory added her own observations about their flight from Hatfield and their sojourn at the Ladle.

"Now we need a bolt-hole," Iris told her old friend, "a place for the hares to hide from the fox, while Northumberland's plot plays itself out. We think Mary and her lords will outfox the fox."

Thorpe often nodded with understanding as Iris and Mallory talked. When they had told their stories, he pushed back his bench and stood. "Well done, my girls," he said. "You're your father's daughter, Iris. But surely you didn't come afoot. Your horses?"

"By the little spring."

"Cover that red hair o' yours, and fetch 'em down."

"But, Thorpe—"

"You're my granddaughters, come to keep a sad old man company," said Thorpe. "Go on. Fetch down the horses. We're going to live, and not in fear, lest Northumberland win everything."

Mallory and Iris retrieved their horses from the little spring in the wood and rode down toward the stableyard. Iris's face was a painful mask of tension, her breakfast a lump in her belly. Hiding now in her own home—what a bitter turn. Surely somebody would recognize her, even with her hair caught back under her cap or a calico scarf. Surely spies would carry the tale back to Northumberland: Iris Bentham had returned to her parents' home with vengeance in her heart. On the Tower of London's green, she would mount the scaffold and kneel to place her head and shoulders on the chopping block.

Shuddering aside these gruesome imaginings, Iris pulled herself up straight in the saddle and walked her horse down to the stables, just as if she weren't atremble. Thorpe came out to greet her and Mallory, as if they hadn't been in conversation an hour earlier, as if, indeed, he hadn't seen them in months.

"My granddaughters!" he called to the stable boys and milkmaids and goose girls and gardeners who worked nearby.

They gathered, taking the horses' reins as Iris and Mallory dismounted. Here was Marcus the cowherd's son, with a little wink for Iris.

There stood Morton, the man who had hung the ropes from the oak for Iris's swing. "You're safe with us," he murmured. So Thorpe already had told them of her fears.

Bessie, the ruddy mistress of the dairy, kissed Iris on the cheek. "Glad to see you gettin' on so well, my lady."

A few of the workers looked up and nodded or smiled, people Iris didn't recognize, and then went on working. Iris turned toward the house, where James and Simon hurried down the path. She had seen them last in the night long months ago, when they helped Thorpe send her away to William Cecil. Now they stopped abruptly and began to converse with each other. A sharp-faced stranger approached the cluster of servants and Iris. He flaunted a sky-blue doublet trimmed in gold and red, as if he were at court.

"The duke's man. Our new *overseer*." Bessie managed to make her whispering sarcastic.

"Northumberland, Thorpe? Is he here?" Iris asked in a low voice.

"Nay, Iris." Thorpe drew her close.

"Your lordship," Thorpe called heartily to the fellow. "My granddaughters, come to Lucy. Pray let me introduce you."

Mallory stepped in front of Iris, blocking her view, but Iris moved to face the man, willing herself to smile and show him her teeth. Shivering though she was, she would not cower.

"See they don't keep you from your work, Thorpe," the man said. "Or eat too much. Let them earn their keep."

He turned abruptly and walked away across the yard toward the pasture, making a show of his indifference to the workers' doings. Iris shook her fist at his back. The old easy manner between master and servants, the sense of a shared home, was gone then as well, dead with the Earl and Countess of Bentham.

THIRTEEN

ucy," Iris said. "Please, Thorpe."

"She's but Lucy's shadow."

"Take me to her."

"I fear to see her myself. Just a minute more to enjoy the sight of you."

Iris headed toward the house, never looking back to see whether Thorpe would follow. Leaving Mac in the yard, she went into the side entrance and down the stairway that led to the kitchen and the kitchen workers' rooms. Everything there was the same as ever. Oil landscapes Mother had bought in the Low Countries hung on the whitewashed walls among paintings of fullblown roses and mixed bouquets—art only slightly inferior to the pictures that hung upstairs in the manor house, and lovely all the same. The familiar scent of slate dust from the floors and of roasting joints of beef perfumed the air. The clang of pots and the whish of knives being sharpened would have led Iris to the kitchen, even if she hadn't known the way.

Cook bent over the marble kneading stone, working a pastry at the great center table, smudges of flour on her cheek and forehead. "And who might you be, bursting into my kitchen without leave?" She pushed a lock of white hair off her face with her forearm.

Since others were working across the kitchen, Iris restrained her pleasure at seeing the old lady she had known all her life. "Thorpe's granddaughter, come to see Lucy."

Thorpe puffed into the kitchen.

"Take your stable boots straight back where you come from," Cook commanded.

"Left 'em at the door," said Thorpe. "I would no more track dirt in here . . ."

None of the scullions was near enough to hear. "Oh, Cook," Iris said in a low voice. "'Tis I!" She whisked her kerchief off her head, letting her red curls drop to her shoulders.

"No! I never! I never thought to see you more!" Cook exclaimed, wiping her floury hands on her apron and rushing around the table to envelop Iris in her arms.

Iris bent to kiss her, but already Cook was whispering

something. "Careful, my lady. Spies is everywhere." She tipped her head toward the great hearth, where a yellow-haired girl pushed a great wooden spatula loaded with loaves of bread into one of the ovens. "That'n there is one," she whispered.

Her elation subdued, Iris covered her hair again.

"Well, Thorpe," Cook went on in a hearty voice. "Your granddaughter. Pity how she'll find our Lucy."

Thorpe was already gone. "Down the way there," said Cook, pointing with her chin. "Robinson put her in her own bed—sleeps by her on a pallet, does Robinson. Tends to Lucy when I can spare her."

Good old Robinson, who had assisted Cook longer than Iris had lived.

Hobbling in his stocking feet, Thorpe was halfway down the passage to Robinson's room. Iris picked up her skirts and ran to catch up with him. Incessant coughing echoed in the hall, the sort of cough that shakes an invalid's lungs and belly and toes and soul.

Thorpe knocked. Robinson opened the door wide. "My granddaughter," he said, looking past Robinson like a sleep-walking man. "Here for Lucy."

Robinson looked up into Iris's eyes. Startled, she inspected her for a moment, and then embraced her. "I'd know you anywhere, my girl."

Iris followed Thorpe to Lucy's bedside. Spots of color reddened Lucy's cheeks, but otherwise her skin was nearly as sallow as the eggshell linen sheets; her lips were blue. Thorpe knelt beside the bed and brushed back her damp hair with his great paw. "'Tis Edward, my beauty. Somebody's here to see you." He made room for Iris.

She leaned over and kissed Lucy's forehead and spoke into her ear. "'Tis Iris, home at last."

Lucy rasped a torturous cough and struggled to speak. Her eyelids fluttered. "Never taunt me, Robinson," she whispered. "They killed her."

"No, Lucy. I escaped. Look at me." Off came Iris's head covering again.

Lucy opened blue eyes that were faded and milky now. She turned her head and struggled to focus on Iris's face. With wonder, she lifted her trembling hand to Iris's hair, then let it drop back to the bed and closed her eyes again, as if seeing were too much effort. Tears flowed down her face and ran onto the pillow as Iris put her old nursemaid's hand to her mouth and kissed it. She had come back to Thorpe and Lucy, only to find them wrecked as thoroughly as Iris was herself.

Another seizure of coughing racked Lucy's body as she tried to speak. Iris put her face close to Lucy's. "My Edward," Lucy whispered. "Look after him."

"We do, and we shall," said Iris.

"Cold." Lucy's teeth chattered, and her body shook with chills.

Iris moved Lucy to the far side of the bed to make room for herself. Turning back the covers and removing her shoes, she slipped into bed beside Lucy. She pulled the down comforter over them both, bundled it under the old woman's chin, and drew her into her arms, shocked by how little she weighed. Iris would warm her dear Lucy with her own body.

The door latch clicked. When Iris looked up, Thorpe and Robinson had left the room.

The following morning, Lucy Thorpe died. Iris and Thorpe and Robinson stood over her washed body, held each other, and wept. The coffin stood ready in the estate carpenter's shop, built days ago to Lucy's measure. Northumberland's overseer paid no notice when, that afternoon, Thorpe hitched Courage and Hope to a farm wagon and drove his wife's body to St. Agnes's Church. Iris and Mallory, Simon and James and Robinson, and several others of the old estate workers followed on foot. They said good-bye to Lucy in the churchyard, as the priest chanted the Protestant funeral rite and buried her in consecrated ground.

The mourners returned to Linnetwood in the wagon, Iris seated beside Thorpe, silently sorrowing for Lucy's death and glad that her suffering had ended. The bright afternoon sunshine felt inappropriate to the day's events, the birdsong an affront. Iris averted her eyes when they approached the drive that led to the house, unable to stomach another glimpse of Northumberland's yellow-and-green coat of arms. She tried to beat down the rage that might expose her and endanger everyone who had hidden her, but it swelled in her gullet nonetheless. As they passed through the gate, she abruptly stood up in the wagon bed. Unable to contain her true self another moment, she raised her fists as far above her head as she could reach and roared.

Thorpe reined in the horses gently, lest Iris lose her balance and fall should they stop suddenly. He put his hand on her shoulder and pulled her down beside him. He took her in his arms and let her weep.

For months she had waited and ached for home, and now Lucy had died at their reunion. Iris wept for Mother and Father. She wept for the workers who had lost the comfort of secure places in a happy home. She wept for the king, dead in his boyhood. She wept for Princess Mary, whose crown Northumberland had stolen, and for poor Jane Grey, whom he had burdened with it. She wept for Princess Elizabeth, bred and born and reared in danger.

Iris wept for herself.

At last, she wiped her face with her homespun skirts and turned around to the others. Their faces, all of them, were awash in tears as well. Simon held up his hand to Iris. She matched her hand to his, palm to palm. She brushed Mallory's fingertips with her own. Then Thorpe clucked to the horses and continued their journey home.

For Iris and Thorpe, the next ten days were joyful, despite their grief. Iris used the practical arts she had learned at Cook's elbow at the Red Lion Inn, preparing simple meals as tasty and nourishing as those Lucy had once cooked for her. Under Iris's affectionate care, Thorpe began to thrive again.

He first drank milk and chicken broth as his stomach recovered from abuse, then ate cheese and eggs, then pig's foot stew. He continued to sleep in the stables, so Iris and Mallory could stay in his rooms, but now his strongest drink was cider at meals. Once again he wore clean clothing every morning.

Mallory asked to labor in the stable, eager to keep busy and fit in, obeying Thorpe's directions in the care of Shadow, Iris's horse. Soon he could exercise in the stableyard. Soon he carried Iris bareback to the pasture, where she galloped him to the far hedgerow for old time's sake before she released him to frolic with the other horses. They greeted him cantering, their tails held high. One noonday, picking daisies and blue catmint and pink phlox for the table after a soft summer morning, Iris realized that her fearful looks over her shoulder had ceased. She had not thought of Northumberland once since breakfast.

That very evening a troop of four horsemen clattered into Linnetwood's courtyard. They bore banners embroidered with interlocked initials: MR. Mary Regina. Queen Mary.

Mary had won.

Thorpe stood with Iris and Mallory and Mac among the lilac bushes at the edge of the courtyard, where they could see and hear without being seen, as Mary's men arrested the defeated Northumberland's underlings. The sharp-featured manager of the estate came slowly out of the house to surrender, wearing another courtly suit of clothes. Iris thought she would faint. Thorpe propped her up as she watched the man who perhaps had arrested her father and mother, who certainly had tyrannized their workers, being arrested himself.

"Long live our good Queen Mary!" said the chief officer of the troop, greeting Northumberland's man with a laugh. "You wagered on the wrong horse, my man."

Recognizing the officer's voice, Iris peered more carefully at him. Sir Andrew, Lord Curlilocks himself. And what was this odd sensation in her chest, this sense that her heart was a bird in flight? Still, Iris huddled in the shadows.

"Ha!" said Thorpe. "There goes Northumberland's treasurer, slinking through the corn. His secretary! That sour old jackdaw of a housekeeper!"

Iris looked behind her. All the ill-tempered people who had seized the rightful places of the Benthams' loyal servants, all the enemies Iris had avoided in recent days, were scuttling away. Northumberland's partisans had scattered, fleeing across the fields and into the wood.

"Sir Andrew Larkin," said Curlilocks, "in the service of Princess Elizabeth. Commissioned by Queen Mary to take into custody Northumberland's agents in this house." Sir Andrew addressed Simon, Father's former secretary. "My men shall deliver them to the Tower of London, with the rest of the traitors."

Iris could hardly contain her triumph. Mary had won indeed. And if Mary had won, then Princess Elizabeth was free. If Princess Elizabeth was free, then Iris was safe as well. She would regain her father's estate. She would live openly again, as herself, in her own home. She could go to London and see Northumberland beheaded.

As soon as the thought of London passed through her

mind, Iris knew that she would be content to let Queen Mary punish the duke without aid from Iris herself. Her vengeful feelings had been thin gruel for her spirit.

Sir Andrew looked about him. "Kindly direct me to the mistress of Linnetwood."

"He knows full well my mother is dead!" sputtered Iris, her face close to Thorpe's ear.

"Sad to say, she is," Thorpe said, "but Iris, the gentleman has come for your father and mother's heir. For you."

Thorpe touched his forehead to salute Iris.

She faltered. Thorpe cocked his elbow, and Iris took it. Together they emerged from the shelter of the lilac bushes.

Sir Andrew had dismounted. For a moment, his horse blocked Iris's view of him. As a stableman led the horse away, Iris approached from behind and touched Sir Andrew's arm. Thorpe stepped back with Mallory.

Andrew's eyes softened. "Thank heavens you're safe, Iris!" As if his hands and arms were acting without his say-so, he reached for her, then caught himself and pulled away. "I am charged to deliver you to Hatfield Royal Palace."

"What? Do not toy with me, sir."

All around, the circle of old Linnetwood servants bent forward, straining to catch every subtle gesture and every word.

Sir Andrew lowered his voice. "I do not jest. Elizabeth would have you by her. Think, Iris, if you are by her, you will be near me." His eyes sparkled with humor.

"I would be near neither of you," Iris said. "I have only just regained my home. I won't go."

"You must. None of us is at liberty to do as we would." Andrew hesitated. "Linnetwood is the property of the crown."

So it was, for now, but Iris would have again what was hers by right.

FOURTEEN

"I must smile and curtsy and wheedle Princess Elizabeth to wheedle and beg and charm Queen Mary to give me my due," Iris sputtered next morning. "Will you stay here for a time, Mallory? Thorpe needs my care. Would you help him in my place?"

"Don't you even care about my lady, Iris? Since Andrew brought the news, you have asked not a single question about the princess."

Mallory's question and the harsh tone in which she

asked it shook Iris. Mallory was right. Had Iris grown callous? "I . . . I . . . Tell me, then, Mallory. Did they catch her?"

Mallory's voice softened. "No, Iris. Thanks to you and your courage, they did not. Andrew told me the duke's lackeys pursued us for days. By the time they realized we had gulled them, they were too late. Elizabeth never left Hatfield."

"What of Sir Jeremy? Kate Ashley and the others?"

"Arrested," said Mallory. "But soon released."

"I care for them all," said Iris. "I do, but Thorpe is on my mind."

"I shall do as you ask—remain here for a few days. You should understand, though, Iris—I belong with Princess Elizabeth, and care for her, as you belong at Linnetwood, and care for Thorpe."

Iris nodded and turned away.

"Have you considered, Iris, that you have no authority here?"

"Authority!" Iris shook both fists over her head. "I shall *take* authority to put things right, until I can sort out my inheritance at court."

"Your chances will be better if the princess stands behind you."

Iris knew the weakness of her position. She must rein herself in, for Sir Andrew had brought a letter in Elizabeth's own hand with a request that amounted to a command. Would Iris return to Hatfield Royal Palace to receive personally the thanks she was due? Iris had no choice; when the heir to Queen Mary's throne summoned, one obeyed.

Preparing to leave Linnetwood once again, Iris found she

had outgrown all her gowns. She dressed in the brown silk that had been Mother's traveling outfit; the gown was too full in the bosom and waist, so she stitched it to fit, using the needle she had carried so long in the hem of her skirt. Now she left the needle where it belonged, piercing the silver-and-velvet pincushion in the old beechwood sewing chest. She packed her mother's favorite blue silk gown and a night-dress for the journey; she might have to stay at Hatfield overnight.

The following morning, Thorpe saddled Shadow.

"What of Hope and Courage, our good horses and saviors?" asked Iris.

"I shall bring them with me when I return to Hatfield," said Mallory.

Iris knelt to tousle MacTavish's silky hair. Thorpe embraced her and spoke into her ear. "Come back."

"Keep well," she said. "I promised Lucy I would look after you. Do that for me. Look after yourself, until I can keep my promise."

"I shall."

Iris sat her horse and gazed across the near meadows, wrenched by the need to leave her home again. Well, she thought, at least she wouldn't be riding with onions in a cart.

"Come," called Sir Andrew.

He was already mounted. His companions had departed for London the day before with their prisoners. Iris rode out at the young knight's side. He tried to gallop away from her, but she spurred Shadow to keep up with him, riding as well as he.

"You mustn't compete with your betters," he called to her over his shoulder.

Iris rode on as if she hadn't heard, refusing to be drawn into an argument.

"Talk to me, Sir Andrew," she said, coming abreast with him again.

"You have fallen rather steeply, in the equestrian realm, since White Rose was your mount."

"Indeed. And you have risen rather far, in the courtly realm, carrying Queen Mary's banner."

"Would that it were Queen Elizabeth's."

"Indiscretion might cost your head one day, sir."

Iris and Sir Andrew surprised a hind, drinking with her well-grown fawn from a rill in the ditch. The deer leapt up onto the roadway and disappeared into the woods on the other side.

"Tell me, what has happened in the world since I left it back at the Ladle?"

"An army gathered around Mary," Sir Andrew said. "Farmers with hoes and scythes. Noblemen with swords. Northumberland led his army out to meet them. But when he left London, his soldiers stole away in the night, and his councilors read the future on his backside. They abandoned his cause."

Iris laughed.

"They arose against him and pronounced Mary Queen of England," Sir Andrew continued.

"What of poor Jane Grey?"

"The nine-day queen—imprisoned now in the Tower."

"Northumberland?"

"Likewise. With his sons."

"Elizabeth?"

"Sharper than ever, and wary of her sister."

They rode on quietly for a time. Above the road ahead, a falcon plummeted down the sky and struck a skylark in midair, scattering its feathers with the force of the blow. A bit of down caught in Iris's eyelash. She pinched the bloody fluff in her fingers and gazed at it, then blew it away on the breeze.

"What happened to you after you left the world at the Ladle?" Sir Andrew asked, glancing at Iris. "I see that Mallory no longer governs you."

"She never did," said Iris. "We stopped in the wood. We ate. We drank. We rode. We arrived home in time for me to bury my nursemaid. I began to be happy again. Then you arrived."

Sir Andrew whooped. "You are a thistle, you are!"

They passed a Roman Catholic priest, wearing a worn and faded cassock, begging in the road. Around the bend, two nuns, dressed in their dusty black habits, walked at the wayside, their rosaries looped at their waists. Iris stared at these strange sights, Catholics openly announcing their religion in their clothing. For some twenty years, since King Henry had put down the Roman Church and placed himself at the head of a new English church, priests and nuns had hidden themselves and their identities.

"News has wings. Already the papists are showing themselves again," Andrew muttered, "now that Mary is in the saddle."

"They say King Edward forbade her to attend mass, on pain of death," Iris said. "Her own brother, Sir Andrew."

"Pardon a correction, my lady. It was Northumberland," he said. "Northumberland made King Edward's decisions at the end."

For all the gossip at the Red Lion, Iris had rarely spoken to a court insider since she left William Cecil's house, not until she met Princess Elizabeth. How good it was to talk again with someone who knew about the sophisticated world, though arrogance tinged everything Curlilocks said.

"What do you suppose will happen now, Sir Andrew?"

"Plain Andrew, my lady," he replied.

"Iris," she said.

"Princess Elizabeth fears Mary. She will certainly reestablish the old religion. She may even cram it down Princess Elizabeth's throat. How many she will slaughter to avenge her Catholic friends' deaths, who can say?"

Mary's mother—divorced and shunned, so that her father could marry Elizabeth's mother. Mary herself, reduced in rank and disowned. Their Catholic friend Cardinal Pole, banished. Iris spat on her fingertips and rubbed the skylark's blood off on her skirt. How, indeed, would Mary take revenge?

"Our fathers—we ourselves," Andrew was saying, "—owe our great estates to King Henry's seizure of the monasteries' lands."

"Folk say that the blood of seventy thousand Englishmen is on his hands. Many were Catholics."

They rode in the shadow of oak trees that were older than the ancient monasteries and churches. Iris glanced at her companion. He wore his dark curls loose about his face, continuous with the neatly trimmed beard and mustache that grew thick, even though he could not have been more than twenty-five. He met her eyes and grinned—he had caught her admiring him. Iris looked away in embarrassment.

"You needn't lecture me on English history, Andrew, nor on the seizure of lands," said Iris, but a wave of guilt drowned her. Then sadness. Then fear. "What if she restores the estates to the Church?"

Andrew laughed. "She won't. Mary needs loyal noblemen. She wouldn't dare reduce us to our fathers' mere former wealth." He had hardly paused before answering; perhaps, like Iris, he had worried about this possibility before.

"Yes," said Iris. "Even the Catholic nobles would rebel against that."

"Countess and knight, the children of nobles," Andrew went on ruefully. "We owe our grand position in part to theft."

He was ridiculing her again. "Stop!" said Iris. "You know perfectly well that Northumberland stripped my parents of their titles. You yourself remind me that Linnetwood is the property of the crown. Am I a lady or am I not? Bother! I hardly know what I am, or who." She spurred her horse, lest he see her face.

Behind her, Andrew laughed. "'Tis all the same to me," he called.

Was his banter ridicule or flirtation?

C⨍⨍⤳

They rested and watered the horses at a small inn. Iris groaned as she dismounted, saddlesore and weary. The innkeeper's maid gave them basins of water for washing the dust from their faces and hands. Despite their fatigue, as soon as they had eaten their bread and cheese and cider, off they went on the road again. They spent the night at another inn, in much less splendor than at the Ladle or even the Red Lion. Iris took supper alone in her room, grateful for quiet and uninterrupted rest.

The next morning, though, as they started off once more, Iris scratched at her back and one leg as energetically as a dog scratching fleas.

Andrew laughed. "Bedbugs, Countess. They love noble blood."

"The servants at the Lion assured me they bite only the sweetest flesh," Iris replied. "I suppose they do not trouble you."

Andrew laughed again. "And I shan't worry that you have many bites. The first bug would have warned the others."

The riders passed the Lion a little after noon. "When I was Cecil's messenger," said Iris, "that is where I worked. An egg girl, you'll remember. Did you know about me? Before, I mean."

"You never saw me there, watching you?"

"Never. I should not have forgotten that smirk, my lord."

Arriving at Hatfield in late afternoon, they rode to the stableyard, dismounted, and left their horses to the grooms. Then they went to the well to wash and drink a sweet draft of water. They entered the palace through the kitchen, where Iris glanced about, looking for the sly girls, especially the serving maid spy, among the scullions who prepared meat and trimmed greens on side tables at the edges of the great room.

"Oh, my lady," Cook called from her oak table in the center, where she was rolling out pastry. "Welcome back. Sit a time."

She pointed at two stools. Iris and Andrew drew them up to Cook's table as she put cheese and mugs of cider before them.

"Food has never tasted better," said Andrew.

"You needn't look behind you anymore," Cook huffed to Iris. "Them spies—thrown out o' the house on their treacherous arses. They'll have a pretty job of work to find another place hereabouts."

"What has happened here, since last we met?" asked Iris.

"Messengers in and out, guests from London—his worship, William Cecil, and who all else?—so many we can't see straight for cooking. Our Elizabeth came out of her apartment and showed herself again when Mary was proclaimed."

"More cheese, if you please," said Andrew. "Nothing like a couple of days' ride to whet one's appetite. And a slab of bread and butter?"

Now that Iris's eyes had adjusted from the bright sunlight to the kitchen's dimness, the bustle was evident. By the wall, a maid flopped a plucked goose into a huge wooden bowl, atop a pile of other gutted and naked fowl, ready to be threaded onto the spits across the fireplace or roasted in pans in the oven. A half-bushel basket had been tipped sideways on another table, spilling small onions from it, their tops still green.

Another maid leaned back from her work, wiping her eyes on her sleeve as she peeled the onions and dropped them into an iron pot. Assistant cooks stirred batter and drizzled honey and severed joints of beef from a hanging carcass. A dozen loaves of bread stood rising, nearly ready for the oven. No wonder sweat-dampened tendrils had sprung loose from Cook's cap and curled on her forehead and neck. Supper was in the making for Elizabeth's household of more than a hundred people.

"The princess sent for me," said Iris. "I must find her now."

"Look again in the arbor—she's either there or a-horseback. Cooped up for days—couldn't even stand at the windows for a breath of air. She sometimes sleeps under netting in the arbor or the woods now. I'm afeared they'll murder her."

Iris and Andrew went around the side of the palace and through the gardens, glad for a walk on solid ground. They found Princess Elizabeth in the arbor, as Cook had thought, walking up and down with a gentleman in the cool shade of the vines and roses. Lettice and Margaret sat on a bench nearby. When she saw Iris and Andrew, the princess spoke a word to her companion, a man dressed for court, who bowed and backed away before he turned to go to the palace. His deference acknowledged that Elizabeth was now immediate heir to the throne, second in the realm only to Queen Mary.

"Sir Andrew," Elizabeth called down the graveled path. "You've brought her." She glowed with vitality as she hurried toward them, catching her red hair up with one hand behind her head, a delighted smile on her long, narrow face.

Andrew bowed with a straight knee in front of him and a courtly sweep of his arm, and Iris curtsied low.

Jumping up, Lettice ran to Iris, and Margaret followed. "You made fools of the duke's dogs, Iris!"

Iris laughed. "They never caught a glimpse of us. What happened after we left the Ladle?"

Margaret rubbed her upper arm and grimaced. "The bruises have healed now."

"They beat Andrew and Jeremy until they couldn't walk," Lettice went on, gazing at Andrew with admiration. "None of us betrayed you and the princess."

Iris stared at Andrew. She had undervalued him, as she had Mallory. She had cared too little about his fate in her concern for her own and Thorpe's.

Before Iris could speak, however, Elizabeth joined them. "You may go, my lord, with my gratitude," she said to Andrew. "I shall see you at supper. And you ladies, too."

Alone now with Iris, Elizabeth shifted a book from her right hand to her left. Then she took Iris by the elbow. "You found me reading last time, too," she said to Iris. "Mr. Chaucer's tales from Canterbury, as I recall." She held up the book she carried now, bound in red leather, with the name of the ancient Greek poet Homer tooled on the cover. *The Iliad,*" she said. "Do you know it?"

"Yes," said Iris. "My father taught me Greek. I read *The*

Iliad with him when I was fourteen, just before—it was the last book we ever read together." Her thoughts silenced her for a moment. "Are you enjoying it?"

"I am taking lessons from King Priam's mistakes. Beware of Greeks bearing gifts," said Elizabeth with a wry laugh. "My sister wants me to come to court. I must prepare myself, and Homer is advising me."

Iris remembered the story of the Trojans' undoing. The Greeks gave them the gift of a gigantic wooden horse on wheels, which the Trojans rolled inside their gates. In the darkness that night, Greek soldiers crept from their hiding place within the horse and opened the gates of Troy to the Greek army. They slaughtered King Priam and the rest of the Trojans, who had been so vain and greedy as to accept gifts from an enemy's hand.

"Queen Mary's invitation is a gift?"

"So she claims. I myself think my royal sister wants to keep me near to hand, the better to watch me."

They walked to the bench where Iris had first found the princess. How strange to be arm in arm with the heir to the English throne so soon after having been an egg girl. How fortune had shifted in just a few weeks! But surely the princess wasn't looking for friendship in a girl she hardly knew, flattering as the attention might be. Surely Iris hadn't been called to Hatfield merely to receive thanks that could as well have been conveyed by letter. What sort of gift was the princess's warmth?

They sat down together and leaned back against the wrought-iron roses and vines. Iris waited for Princess

Elizabeth to speak, but she did not. Elizabeth waited too, scanning the sky. Skylarks sang somewhere, and swallows darted after insects, flying away again when their beaks bristled with tiny legs and wings. Iris imagined a falcon roosting somewhere hidden and high, awaiting opportunity. As the afternoon waned, gray clouds dulled the sky. A wind whipped up, promising rain on the morrow, if not this very evening.

The rainy return to Linnetwood on horseback would be uncomfortable, then, but not uneasy like this silence. Iris longed to be away. She smoothed her mother's traveling gown, fidgeting, brushing off real and imaginary dirt, though the heathery silk did not show the dust of the road.

What could Princess Elizabeth want?

Iris glanced at the elder girl, trying to read her mind. Elizabeth would soon be twenty years of age. She was not a girl at all, but a woman now, of a proper age for marriage and children. She looked back at Iris through amused and narrowed eyes, her chin tipped up. As she had that morning in her rooms before asking Iris to decoy Northumberland's men away from Hatfield, Elizabeth measured Iris again. The way a fox enjoys the prospect of a tasty rabbit, Iris thought, or a falcon assesses a lark.

"Lovely day, isn't it?" said Elizabeth.

"Oh, yes, it was a lovely cool day for travel." Lovely day? Had Iris been summoned here to talk of the weather?

The wind huffed, ruffling the leaves of the arbor roses.

"Or it was, at least," said Elizabeth, "before those clouds hid the sun. But I am so grateful for a breath of air that I would sit here out-of-doors through a whirlwind."

"I fear I shall have to ride in the rain tomorrow."

"We shan't travel tomorrow," said Elizabeth.

"I should like to return to my home as soon as possible."

"Yes. I quite understand. Your home." With an emerald jewel in the shape of a bird, Elizabeth pinned back a strand of red hair that the wind had loosened. "Tell me, Iris: Have you any male relatives?"

"No. Not one. My mother gave birth to six boys, but those who were born alive all died before the age of two. I was the only girl. Only I survived childhood."

"No uncles?"

"My mother had a brother, but all my father's brothers were killed in the Duke of Somerset's Scottish war. Three in one day, dead in a single battle."

"Ah. War. Our eternal companion, along with pestilence, starvation, and human perfidy." Elizabeth sighed. "Then you would have inherited your father's estate, had Northumberland not seized it."

"Oh, yes," said Iris. "It would have been mine now."

"As the property of a traitor, it reverted to the crown. You are legal ward of the crown."

"Yes, but my father was no traitor." Iris's heart thudded in her chest and her ears.

"Of course not, but Northumberland was," Elizabeth said. "And after your parents died, my brother, King Edward, settled their estate on him." She smiled. "A little reward for services rendered, my brother doubtless thought."

What was this conversation about? Had Elizabeth called

Iris here to declare what she already knew, to her heartache—that she was bereft of everything?

"Sir Jeremy has told me of your boldness," Elizabeth went on, "in leading Northumberland's men a merry chase away from the Ladle. I am grateful to you."

"I served you faithfully well before that," said Iris, her resentment rising to crowd out confusion. "From the day William Cecil placed me at the Lion, I risked my life to be your messenger."

"Yes, I know. You are just the sort I need about me. You do as I ask you, yet you think for yourself. You show courage and backbone. Your intelligence shines in you. Where is my lady Mallory, by the by?"

"I asked her to stay at Linnetwood and look after my responsibilities until my return."

"She must come here to Hatfield. I have need of her. My household moves to London in one week's time. Mary requires us to take up residence at my palace in London, Somerset House."

What had this news to do with Iris? She was sick to death of everyone's ordering her about, but she feared this royal falcon. If Elizabeth insisted she serve at court, must she obey the heir to the throne? So she must, but she must also return to Linnetwood and set things right. She must tarry on the swing that hung in the oak tree at the side of the house, and take time to think and plan. She must tend Lucy's grave and see to Thorpe. She couldn't—

"The breeze has stiffened," said Elizabeth. "Go to the house now. Get rid of that ugly gown, wash off the horse sweat, and eat a hot meal. I cannot be served by ragamuffins—ask Mrs. Ashley to give you one or two of my old gowns. We shall talk again before long."

Princess Elizabeth stood abruptly, *The Iliad* under her arm. She gestured toward the palace with her hand, as one shoos a dog.

FIFTEEN

aughter and loud voices and music floated to Iris from the people gathered for supper in Elizabeth's rooms. Iris had not been invited to join them, nor did she wish to go. Instead, she took supper alone in the same room where she had slept before, and was told to remain there until she was summoned. She would have given anything to be back at Linnetwood, in Thorpe's and Lucy's cozy rooms. Her isolation here felt like prison.

Katherine Ashley herself brought breakfast next morning,

and dishes enough for two. She sat with Iris at the window overlooking the garden, just as she had before, sharing the food. Rain shrouded the world with low-hanging fog.

"Oh, Kate! What happened to your face?" asked Iris.

A dark brown stripe marred Kate's cheek, like the mark of a lash. Kate fingered the injury. "Just something to remember Northumberland by. It is fading. Now eat, Iris. Then tell me of your adventures." Mrs. Ashley scooped boiled eggs from the shells and buttered them. She poured a tisane of bergamot flowers steeped in hot water. "Here. If you can't eat, drink."

"I left my appetite in the garden yesterday, with the mighty Elizabeth. She spoke obliquely. What does she demand of me now?" Iris sipped the drink as the eggs congealed on the plate. She might have wept, had she been less angry. But no. She would not weep. Instead she would match Elizabeth's imperious spirit.

"The princess is sometimes less considerate than she might be," Mrs. Ashley said. "Less tactful—"

"Considerate! Tactful! I cannot inherit my parents' estate, she gave me to understand. I may not go home. I must continue to serve her, rather than myself." Iris stuffed her wild feelings back down her throat. Her parents had defied the king's men. Iris was but a skylark, like the one the falcon had struck. Her parents' fate could befall her, too.

"She was ever conscious of her rank," Mrs. Ashley said. "But think, Iris. You had your mother and father until you were nearly fifteen. Her father ordered her mother's execution when Princess Elizabeth was but three."

"Yes. I know her history well, for everyone I meet must tell it to me again." Iris stood and gazed down at Hatfield's gardens. "It is bad fortune, I begin to think, to be noble. Born the daughter of a stableman and a nursemaid, I might have been happy. The princess, as well."

"'Tis an honor to be chosen for court."

"'Tis an honor I can do without, Kate. I shall return to the Lion and tend the chickens. And if Queen Mary will not restore Linnetwood to me, I shall go back to it as goose girl." She knew even as she spoke that the crown could prevent her doing anything of the sort.

Katherine Ashley cleared the pewter plates and spoons and knives and piled them back on the tray. "A maid will come for these. Now Princess Elizabeth wishes to speak with you again. Hear her out, my dear." She kissed Iris lightly on the cheek. "Come now."

Iris smoothed the skirt of her mother's blue silk gown, which she had pleated and pinned to fit; she would die before she wore Elizabeth's castoffs. She followed Kate, rubbing the place where she had kissed her, considering how desperate she must be, to be tamed by a kiss on the cheek.

Through several shabby rooms they went, just as they had done a few weeks earlier, through the gallery, and into Princess Elizabeth's sitting room. This time the princess stood alone at the window, leaning her forehead on the thick and wavery glass. She stood there as if she hadn't heard footsteps, watching the rain. Having delivered Iris to the falcon, Mrs. Ashley went out again.

If Elizabeth thought Iris was of use, then Iris might turn

the game to her advantage. Elizabeth was her only hope of regaining her inheritance. She had been an egg girl. She had played counterfeit princess. Surely she could feign pleasure in Elizabeth's service long enough to gain what she desired. Iris would play her own game now.

Eventually, Princess Elizabeth turned to Iris. "Good morning."

Iris curtsied.

"Sit."

Iris sat.

"How do you do today?"

"Well, your Highness."

"It is an uneasy thing to be Mary's heir." Elizabeth sat down in a chair where she could watch the rain stream down the glass. "No sleep last night again. No appetite. I should prefer to be a milkmaid."

Iris sighed. "Neither of us can choose, I see. You no more than I."

"I perhaps even less than you." Elizabeth fingered a worn spot in her wine-velvet cushion. "Mary has hated me since I was born, when she was seventeen. One false move, one mistake, and I shall be dead. I need bright and spirited people near. Will you come to court with me? Just through the summer?"

"Do our hair and height have something to do with your request?"

Elizabeth laughed. "You see. I like your spirit!"

"I want to go home. I have no home." Iris could feign pleasure later; now she must try again for release.

"Come with me. I shall do what I can for you. I promise."

Iris stretched for an excuse not to go. "I have no clothing suitable for court." She held Mother's gown away from her waist, proving how ill it fit.

Elizabeth laughed. "I told you to ask Kate for gowns that I have outgrown. You will not find them too shabby for your taste. . . . I remember a time," she went on, "when Cecil said you wanted vengeance. Vengeance has come. Northumberland now breathes the Tower's fetid air."

Elizabeth threw back her head and studied the ceiling, as if seeing the duke's future written there. "I hope they have housed him near the menagerie. I look forward to festive occasions at the Tower just so I can feed the creatures. Guardsmen say the animals hoot and howl the whole night long. The stench is magnificent."

"What will happen to him?" asked Iris.

"Northumberland? Mark this prophecy, Iris: John Dudley, the self-made Duke of Northumberland, will not see another autumn. Come to London. We shall see him dead together."

The seeming choice Elizabeth offered, to stay or not, was illusory. Iris saw no way out. Nevertheless, the princess already had offered to help her, and—an extra boon—the punishment of her parents' tormentor would satisfy Iris's hatred of him. Thin gruel or no, revenge was what Iris had left.

She took a deep breath, as if diving under water. "I put myself in your hands, but only for the summer," she said. "If we are unhappy at court, we shall steal away together and melt into the countryside. I shall teach you how to work. We shall labor at an inn together, you in the dairy, I in the fowl coops."

The princess's laughter rang down through the connecting rooms. "If only escaping our fate were so easy!"

Iris would go to London and witness at close range the defeat of Northumberland. His defeat, after all, had been what she wanted. Yet her chest felt hollow, heartless, as if the bird within had flown away.

She would go to London, but her heart would be at Linnetwood.

When she returned to her room, Iris saw immediately that her mother's traveling gown was gone. *"Where is it?"*

Her shout echoed through the palace. A maid came running from either direction.

"Where? That gown and this"—Iris held out her blue silk skirt—"are all I have of my mother."

"'Twas sent to be used for rags," said one of the girls, huddling behind a chair and nervously rubbing her chin, transferring onto her face ashes from the hearths she had been cleaning.

"Rags? Rags? Bring it back at once!"

"But, my lady." The girl spoke in a whisper. "I was ordered."

"Who ordered?"

"Why, the housekeeper, my lady."

"Who ordered the housekeeper?"

"I'm sure I wouldn't know, my lady."

"I will have my mother's gown. Where is it?"

"With the laundry, no doubt, my lady."

Iris hurried down the back stairs and out the door into the rain, past the stables, past the dairy, to the place where fires burned all day, every day, for the washing of the palace linens. As she hurtled across the wet slates, holding her skirt hem in her hand, leaping across mud puddles, she absorbed everything she saw in the laundry yard beyond the dairy. Under the protection of a rough roof on posts, to keep the drizzle off, two muscular women stirred the contents of several gigantic, steaming pots. Another twisted the steaming linens, wringing out the hot water, and let the sheets and clothing fall into woven willow baskets. A fourth shook out linens that had already cooled and pinned them to ropes with wooden pegs to dry when the sun came out.

Iris went straight to the great baskets of dirty laundry and threw one piece after another onto the stone floor.

"'Ere, you!" One of the washerwomen seized Iris by the shoulder. Sweat ran down the woman's face, despite the coolness of the day. She smelled of ale. "What're you after, messin' in our work?"

"My mother's gown! I will have my mother's gown."

"Gown? What gown? These 'ere is bedsheets."

So they were, many stained bedsheets, pungent with the odor of many people's bodies. Bed linens at Hatfield Royal Palace were evidently not changed as often as they had been at Linnetwood.

Iris stood with arms hanging at her sides. "My mother's gown. The princess did not like it. The maid took it with the laundry. For *rags*."

The big woman laughed and wiped her face with her apron. "What's gone is gone, then." She turned back to her long stick and the bubbling pot.

"Brown, it is. Heathery silk."

The woman straightened. "No silk hereabouts. Anyhow, my lady, might's well try to turn back the tide as flail against Herself. The princess has her way."

"Go along now," said the other washerwoman. "We've work to do."

Iris would not give up so easily. She ran back to the palace, and raced up the stairs, frantic to find the maid. The girl still toiled on her hands and knees, cleaning a hearth. Iris seized her by the shoulder and flung her around, knocking her off balance. "Where is it, my mother's gown? 'Tis not in the laundry. Where?" Her voice was a howl.

The girl cowered, trembling at Iris's feet, her shoulder hunched to protect her face. Iris turned away and covered her eyes with her hand. What would her mother have thought of such a scene? Lucy? Iris turned back and reached for the girl, who scuttled away.

"No! I shan't hurt you. Let me help you up." Iris pulled the girl to her feet. "What is your name?"

"Mercy," the girl whispered.

"Mercy, indeed. Lord have mercy on us all. Forgive me, Mercy, for I am crazed."

Mother's gown was gone. Iris was powerless to save it. She went back down to the stableyard and ladled water from a bucket to wash the tears from her face. She drank from the ladle, and then entered the stable, where she found her own saddle, clean and polished, in the tack room. Shadow was gone, though, turned out to pasture with all the other horses. Even in William Cecil's study, even at Mrs. Pennefeather's house, even at the Ladle with Sir Jeremy and Mrs. Ashley, Iris had never felt such loss.

SIXTEEN

reparations for moving the field household were already well under way. Of course, the servants were accustomed to such moves. After a few weeks of residence in one of her houses, the princess must move to another, while workers rid the first of fleas, animal waste, and human filth. The local farmers must be allowed to replenish their stocks. King Edward had furnished Somerset House when he deeded it to Elizabeth, but her own and her many servants' clothing and other personal belongings must be packed and transported.

As Elizabeth had promised, Kate provided Iris with gowns. One, made of olive twill, with a gold jerkin and gold sleeves, was suitable for sport. Another was of ruby silk. The third was very fine indeed, shimmering iridescent blue now, and then, when it slightly moved, a lovely opaline green. Lace decorated the low neck and the wrists of the separate sleeves.

Iris hid her mother's blue gown far under the mattress, where no maid would notice it. She would pack it with her other things when the household moved. Although she had vowed she would die rather than wear Elizabeth's castoffs, she must swallow her bile in order to play the game she intended.

Iris had much need of the olive gown, for, while the servants worked, Elizabeth frolicked, and her ladies and gentlemen attended her. Soon Mallory rejoined the household, having been summoned from Thorpe's side at Linnetwood; Andrew had gone to escort her back to Hatfield. Thorpe was safe, Mallory reported, in James's and Simon's hands.

Elizabeth sat a galloping horse better than the men. One early morning, as usual, they raced, they hunted roebuck, they rested, and then they hunted wild boar. At noonday, the kennelmen called in the hounds and fed them. Servants had brought hampers of food and jugs of drink, bright rugs for the ground, and tapestry pillows to lounge on. Such gaiety Iris had not enjoyed in months.

Andrew came to sit beside her. "How did you find my people at Linnetwood when you fetched Mallory? Is my old Thorpe well? Sober?" she asked.

"All is peaceful, now that Northumberland's minions are gone. Mallory says that your father trained his workers well. They know what to do, and they do it without being told."

"Of course my father trained them well!" Iris sputtered.

"Andrew," Elizabeth called. Her noblemen had gathered around her, laughing and leaning back on their elbows, and showing off. "Are you spurning me, Andrew?"

He cleared his throat and growled a bit, low, as a sign to Iris, but he stood and obeyed the summons. Jealousy burned in Iris as Elizabeth flirted with him, and then turned her back on him to flirt with another. The heir to the throne of England had a power that the chroniclers rarely marked.

After the meal, the kennelmen set loose the dogs again. They flushed a hind, which the riders pursued pell-mell through the woods, across a glade, and into a pond. As the deer stood trembling in breast-deep water, its eyes wild and its mouth open, gasping for air, Elizabeth drew her bow and aimed an arrow at its heart. Iris held her breath.

The princess relented and lowered her bow. "Catch her for me," she ordered her men.

Andrew and Sir Jeremy splashed into the water with four others, surrounded the poor creature, and, laughing, wrestled her onto the bank of the pond.

Elizabeth dismounted from White Rose. Seizing the hilt of the knife she carried at her waist, moving quick as lightning, she cut off one of the hind's ears with a smooth and sudden motion. "Ho!" she shouted. Her eyes sparkling, she held the ear aloft. "Now the beast has given up a trophy—let her go!"

The men stood away. The hind leapt free of the crowd and

escaped into the wood, blood streaming down her throat. Everyone, even gentle Mallory, cheered and imitated the princess, fists thrusting into the air as if they too held an ear, and laughed at the merry sport. Everyone but Iris. She shuddered and lay down along Shadow's neck, her head between the horse's ears, to collect herself. What sort of person was this princess, peremptory one day, pensive the next, vicious the third?

Elizabeth hooted. "Come, Iris, surely you've seen worse butchery than mine," she called. "Come, take my trophy— keep it for me—carry it back to the house in your pocket."

"I am unwell," said Iris. She flicked the reins and turned Shadow back toward the palace, nausea roiling in her belly.

Mallory immediately caught up with her. "You must stay!" she said. "The princess does not take well to insolence."

Iris removed Mallory's hand from the rein and stared her former companion in the eyes. Then she nudged Shadow with her heels and rode away. At the palace, she asked for books and herbal tea and shut herself in her room. She would enjoy no more hunting here. No more privileges at all, not if she could help it.

Within a week, Iris's joining the hunt was no longer at issue, for the household had moved from Elizabeth's country estate at Hatfield to Somerset House in London. Given a room overlooking the gardens again, and the riverbank, Iris was grateful for the beauty Elizabeth or Kate Ashley or some other kind soul had afforded her. She found as she explored the mansion that some corridors were locked or boarded up.

"The palace lost its patron," Kate Ashley explained. "King Edward's uncle, the Duke of Somerset, built this house while he was lord protector. He was beheaded, and Northumberland gained authority in his place, before Somerset ever could move in."

Iris saw how things had been. Somerset's death had ended construction of the house, and Northumberland had not cared to complete his predecessor's grand plans. Neither the furnishings nor the house itself were as fine as those at Linnetwood.

On her first day in London, Iris went outdoors to cut some flowers, hoping to escape captivity at Elizabeth's elbow. Kate Ashley found her there.

"You must come keep the princess company," Kate said. "That is why she brought you here. Be witty. Sing. Dance. Listen to her conversation."

"Poor company I should be, among those sycophants," said Iris. "They orbit her as if they were moons, and she the sun."

Mrs. Ashley put her hand to her mouth. "You mustn't talk such fiddle-faddle about orbits and suns and moons! Especially with a Catholic queen coming to the throne. The Church burns people for less."

Indeed it did, for the Church held to the ancient belief that the sun orbited the earth rather than the reverse. Churchmen believed the earth was the center of everything, God's chosen place.

"I am talking about sycophants, not about Master Copernicus and his astronomy. I cannot bear these fools."

"In the households of our betters, we must bear what comes, like it or no." Mrs. Ashley turned again at the doorway. "Princess Elizabeth requires you to join the others at her entertainments."

Iris returned to her room, where she found a new gown made expressly for her, this one russet and gold. Russet, she saw in the glass, suited her as well as it did Elizabeth. The knowledge gave her confidence that she needed, for she did join the others, as Kate had ordered her to do.

All that day and evening, except when Elizabeth wanted rest or quiet, Iris stood at the edge of the room until the arches of her feet ached, waiting for Elizabeth to give her leave to sit. She spoke politely when others spoke to her. She bore what she did not like, though she had to admit that the princess's conversation was learned and amusing.

After supper, the music suddenly stopped, and all eyes turned to a man dressed in black velvet and white silk galligaskins, striding across the room toward Elizabeth. William Cecil. He spoke with the princess a moment, then looked around. The princess pointed at Iris. Cecil came smiling to her side, bowed, and kissed her hand. "Ah, my dear Iris, we have much to thank you for."

"You may thank me by arranging my return to Linnetwood," said Iris.

"Umm. Yes. Ever the spitfire." His eyes hardened. "We must wait to see how things sort out. We must be patient."

The music began again, Cecil nodded, bowed, and walked

away. He approached Harriet, the elderly lady who had accompanied Iris to the Ladle with Kate and Mallory and the others. She joined him in a stately dance, but she was limping. Northumberland's curs had beaten her, too.

A few evenings later, excitement buzzed in the air, though Iris could discern no difference except in the company's mood. A quartet sat at a four-sided table, each musician playing from a score placed on its tilted surface. Most of the noblemen and ladies danced, for when the princess danced, she obliged others to do so as well. They were the same ladies as always. The same gentlemen. The same Mallory flirted with the same Sir Jeremy. Yet every person seemed more gay and sparkling, leaping higher in the dance, smiling more broadly, laughing with more abandon.

Andrew approached Iris and observed what was obvious. "You are not dancing."

"I turned my ankle."

"You entered here without a limp."

"I turned my temper, then."

"Have you heard the news from Mary's court?"

"News. No, Queen Mary's courtiers do not report to me. Andrew, I want to go home."

"Her Majesty will enter London tomorrow. She calls for Princess Elizabeth to ride at her side. The rest of us will ride behind Queen Mary's company." Andrew could hardly contain his self-importance. "Did you ever imagine, when you were an egg girl, that you would accompany the Queen of England as she entered London?"

"Never. Andrew, I want to go home," she said again.

Whether the music and gaiety were too loud, or he was too excited, he ignored her lament. "You and I shall ride in the queen's parade—and, Iris, have you heard about Northumberland? The council have tried him and found him guilty of treason. His execution is set for three weeks hence. You shall have your revenge."

An icy thrill ran through Iris's body. "Had Northumberland won, they as easily would have found Queen Mary guilty of treason, and she would be waiting for the chopping block instead. Thank you for the news."

Iris was weak with the nausea that soon came in the wake of the thrill. She arose from her cushion on the floor and stepped quickly away from Andrew. She slipped unnoticed along the gallery wall, through the door, and back through the many large rooms to her own. She hung the russet silk gown on a peg and changed into her nightdress. Though the night was warm, Somerset House, built of stone and located on the riverbank, was damp and chilly. Iris lay down on her bed and pulled an eiderdown coverlet up over her ear, dabbing at her nose with Mother's lace handkerchief. A terrible shudder seized her. Northumberland would be beheaded. In three weeks, his raven-pecked head would join the Earl of Bentham's at the gateway to London Bridge.

Why could Iris not rejoice?

SEVENTEEN

On the morning of Queen Mary's entrance into London, Somerset House was already astir by first light. By ten o'clock, Elizabeth's household had joined Mary's larger troop of attendants outside the city. They were forming a ragged procession, standing about, restless, or lying on the ground, reins in hand, their horses and they themselves growing hungry and thirsty in the summer sun. Iris stood for a long time. Then she sat. At last, tired of waiting, she lay back on a grassy bank beside Andrew, who tried to whistle with a blade of grass.

Iris pulled another blade of grass, held it between her thumbs as her father had taught her, and blew. Her piercing whistle startled the horses and drew the attention of people nearby. Andrew smiled. Iris put her right-hand finger and thumb in her mouth and whistled again.

"For the love of God," shouted a surly-looking man. "Make no more commotion than cannot be avoided!"

Iris and Andrew laughed until they cried.

"What think you of the glorious life of a courtier?" he asked when they had settled themselves again.

"I thought ill of it before you brought me back to the palace. I think less well of it every day."

Iris adjusted the bodice of Elizabeth's iridescent blue gown; this neckline rode too low on her bosom. Beautiful though the gown was, it was only a garment—not so unlike the rough clothing of the egg girl, after all.

Andrew's eyes had followed Iris's fingers to the bosom of the gown. Discovered, he looked away.

He regained his composure in a moment. "You have but tasted the boredom of life in Princess Elizabeth's household," he said. "Think what life at court will be. We shall wait in line and stand at the edges of rooms for the rest of our days."

Andrew brushed Iris's face with an ear of the tall grass that grew at the verge. "One may stay or go only at the will of the king. Well, now the queen. Her attendants may marry only with her permission, and all but the greatest courtiers must leave their wives in the country."

The proud Andrew Larkin was gabbling, his conversation following no logical course. Andrew Larkin was nervous! Iris picked her own ear of grass and tickled him back. "Are you thinking of marriage, Andrew?"

He blushed. Andrew Larkin blushed! Iris had never seen him embarrassed before. "Mother grew lonely at Linnetwood, while Father served at King Henry's court," she said. "Still, she would have preferred the country life even if the king had been willing to house and feed all the hundreds of his noblemen's relatives."

"How may one advance, though, Iris, without the queen's influence?"

"So far has Northumberland advanced that his next stop will be the executioner's block." Iris slapped the ends of the reins on her hand. "The reputation of advancement is a finer thing than its reality."

The people ahead of them in the procession began to stir. Iris and Andrew sat up and looked around.

"You may say so," said Andrew. "You, your father's only child. His heir. I am but a third son. When Father dies, my eldest brother will inherit everything, of course. I shall have to bend to him and call him the earl."

"You must marry well, then, as must I."

"Oh, what shall we do, Iris?" Andrew moaned. "I am as tired of grandeur as you, but Elizabeth is my hope."

"Life in a royal household, it seems, is eight tenths standing around, thumbs a-twiddle; one tenth dancing and hunting; and one tenth terror," said Iris. "I shall find work in the country somehow. I shall be a milkmaid at Linnetwood."

"Pish, Iris, you talk a lot of rot, always feeling sorry for yourself. Really, you should be a lady-in-waiting. You have all the graces." Andrew glanced at her bosom again, then leapt to his feet and fidgeted with his horse's bridle until the red flush on the back of his neck subsided. When he sat down in the grass again, neither he nor Iris looked at the other or spoke.

The sun had climbed high in the sky by the time the people in the distance mounted their horses. The milling animals and people raised a cloud of dust, for the earth was dry again, despite the recent rain. Iris coughed and brushed at a grass stain on the princess's gown. The column of riders moved, Iris and Andrew riding almost at the rear, as befitted their lowly station, starting and halting several times before the line of horses proceeded smoothly.

Iris looked at Andrew. "Like it or no, as Mrs. Ashley says. Like it or no, we are on our way to court and must make the best of it."

As the horses descended a long, gradual hill, passing through the orchards and cropland and berry patches on the outskirts of London, the column snaked visibly ahead, so many horsemen and ladies that Queen Mary and Princess Elizabeth were far out of sight in the distance.

Observing the vista before them, principally the horses' rear ends just ahead, their haunches and swinging tails, Iris snorted. "Magnificent view, isn't it? Magnificent occasion."

One of the horses dropped a great load of manure in the road.

"Such splendor as only the greatest in the land may know." Andrew drew a deep breath of road dust scented with horse manure. "Fresh country air, as well."

By the time Iris and Andrew entered London, the procession of more than one thousand courtiers had been passing any given corner for hours. The streets were strewn with flowers that people had brought to Queen Mary, crushed amid the manure and the missiles small boys threw. Were they garbage, these missiles? Yes—that was a rotten egg that barely missed Iris's nose and splattered on the paving stones as the boy who had thrown it turned and ran. That was a small cabbage that struck the wall of a shop just ahead. A waste of good cabbage, Thorpe would have said. With every step, the horses' hooves scattered the gravel that workmen had used to smooth the road and provide an even path for the queen; now the surface was rough and pocked with ruts and holes.

As the procession's tail of noble underlings approached the Tower, many of the riders veered off, returning to Greenwich Palace, or Hampton Court, or wherever they served. Princess Elizabeth had given orders, however, that Iris and Andrew remain with the others of her household. Her ladies and gentlemen gave her courage, she said.

"Are we Elizabeth's guards, Andrew?"

He patted the hilt of his sword. "I suppose we are."

"I like not this occupation."

They passed through streets lined with ramshackle houses and crowded by urchins. Ragged men and women who might have welcomed the queen had grown tired of the procession's intrusion on their peace. Now sneers distorted their faces, and drink brought their resentment to the surface. A snaggle-toothed man shook an ornate silver cross at the riders, perhaps one stolen from a ransacked Catholic church, which he held contemptuously upside down, declaring himself a Protestant. Neighbors crowded within an arm's length of the ale casks Queen Mary had provided for the celebration, wiping the froth from their mouths on their sleeves. A fat woman fixed Iris with a watery eye, then turned her back, bent over, and lifted her skirt, revealing bare feet, bare legs, bare bottom, bare everything. Her companions' laughter was a rookery's raucous caws.

Iris turned to Andrew, who leaned toward her to hear. "We spend but a tenth of our days in terror now," she said. "Should these people ever think to rise up as one, what proportion then?"

Farther into London, foul odors intensified as the neighborhoods became ever more crowded. Iris held her rose-scented handkerchief to her mouth and nose, trying not to notice the reek of sewage, poured every morning into the streets from the bedchambers above; of privies behind the houses; of rotten fruits and vegetables and offal; of the pigs and chickens that rooted and scratched in the side streets and little gardens beside the main thoroughfare.

"What is this place?" asked Iris, pointing toward a hillside where hundreds had gathered to watch all of England's greatest folk assembled in one line.

"Why, Tower Hill."

Tower Hill. Iris bent low over Shadow's head, as if her

breath had been kicked out of her chest. She had forgotten she would have to pass by Tower Hill and the scaffold where her father had died.

Andrew watched her, a puzzled expression on his face. "You're ill?"

Though she certainly was sick, Iris shook her head. When would she recover from these seizures of grief? How would she gird herself against memory? She commanded herself to sit up again as straight as if she were an ordinary girl, not an orphan borne down by pain. She leaned across the space between her horse and Andrew's and reached for his hand. He took her hand in his and squeezed. Gradually, her stomach settled. She let Andrew's hand go and fixed her eyes on the great riverside fortress.

As the procession passed through the Tower of London's gates, Iris pressed her handkerchief to her face, but the stink overwhelmed the delicate scent of her rosewater.

"What stench is this?" said Iris. "My father's stables are a perfumery by contrast to this place."

"The moat." Andrew pointed toward the river.

A moat surrounded the old walled castle, filled with water from the Thames. As the rising tide flooded upstream and the falling tide roared downstream, the river flushed the moat when it was high. In the heat of July, though, the river itself was none too fresh, and the water level was low. The sewage and garbage and other waste in the moat festered there.

"No wonder the court moves to the country in summer," said Iris, "lest everybody suffocate."

Above the hundreds of horses' clopping hooves and the

creaking of leather saddles and bridles, came a scream, followed by more shrill and foreign sounds.

Iris gestured toward the strange noise.

"The menagerie," said Andrew. "Monkeys. Parrots. Spotted leopards. Whatever strange creatures may be found in Christendom and beyond."

The menagerie. Princess Elizabeth had hoped Northumberland was housed nearby, where the hoots and howls of the creatures might trouble his sleep. A trembling began in Iris's fingers, traveled up her arms and shoulders, and engulfed her whole body.

"What is it, Iris?" Andrew reached for her hand. "We've nothing here to fear."

"Northumberland."

Andrew gasped. "Of course! He's there." Andrew pointed at Beauchamp Tower. "They say he has renounced Protestantism and asked for confession with a priest. 'A living dog is better than a dead lion,' he told his friends."

"He will say and do anything to save himself." Iris stared at Beauchamp Tower. "He thinks Mary will forgive him. What if she releases him? What might he do to me?"

"She would as soon forgive Anne Boleyn," said Andrew. "He's locked up here, along with three of his sons. He is sentenced to death for treason. Smile, Iris. You've won."

Perhaps she had, if any kind of winning could come of dead parents and the loss of their titles and estate. At least she was alive. Northumberland would soon be dead. Iris looked across the Tower of London green to the spot where Anne Boleyn had been beheaded. The wooden scaffold had been erected again, awaiting the duke. He had to have heard the clatter of every plank and the hammering of every nail.

From across the green came Queen Mary's gruff laughter. The feather on Princess Elizabeth's hat bobbed in the crowd. Iris breathed a deep draft of the fetid air. She looked up at the tawny walls of Beauchamp Tower, which overlooked the scaffold. While he waited, Northumberland could look down upon the green and contemplate his own mortality.

Iris's emotions shifted from moment to moment. Now she was gaining courage. She would not be cowed by an imprisoned traitor. Her reins were wrapped around the hand that held the pommel of her saddle. With the other, she waved at Beauchamp Tower's windows and stretched to improve her view. Perhaps she might see Robin Dudley; perhaps, the Duke of Northumberland himself. Her heart pounding with defiance against her breastbone, she blew a mocking kiss.

A shadow moved at an open window, then Northumberland's glowering face appeared, and then the window was empty again.

"Thus may all tyrants die," said Iris, but rage had suffocated her triumph.

After the celebratory feast, Princess Elizabeth's attendants returned with her to Somerset House. The princess dismounted in the courtyard. She handed her hat to Mrs. Ashley, unpinned her red hair, and shook it out, muttering all the while.

"Oh, my darling," said Katherine Ashley. "We must make the best of it."

"Make the best of it, indeed! I want to return to Hatfield, but bear London I must." Elizabeth's voice rose ever louder and higher as she mounted the steps and entered the stone reception hall of Somerset House, surrounded by fluttering, anxious attendants.

The princess's curses echoed off the stone walls. "Mary has commanded me to attend mass with her at Richmond Palace on Sunday."

Mrs. Ashley's words came back to Iris; in the households of her betters, even the princess must bear what came, like it or no.

"I have kept an old rosary that was once your father's," said Kate, patting Elizabeth's arm.

The princess whirled away from the touch. "Stop fussing at me!" she snarled.

Mrs. Ashley and the others shrank away from her, making room as Elizabeth stormed back and forth, pulling at one hand with the other, brushing her hair back violently, dabbing at her nose with a handkerchief.

"Can't you see? Her first act will be to restore the Catholic Church by force! She'll marry a Catholic king. Already she has set her eyes on Philip."

Philip. The King of Spain. Iris looked around for Andrew and found him just behind her. "Remember the nuns and priest on the road?" he said. "They foresaw this day."

Iris took Andrew's arm and repeated to him the name, fraught with heavy history and foreboding: "King Philip of England . . ."

"She will have her revenge on me yet," Elizabeth wailed. "Catherine of Aragon's revenge on Anne Boleyn."

Catherine of Aragon, the Spanish princess, Queen Mary's mother. King Henry had divorced her to marry Anne Boleyn. Mary would avenge her mother, as Iris wished to avenge her own parents. Revenge was not a pretty thing.

Andrew bent to Iris's ear. "If the King of Spain becomes the King of England . . ." he said.

Iris completed his sentence. ". . . Mary's realm will be but a Spanish colony." Queen Mary's revenge would mean a bitter future for Elizabeth and her partisans, for King Philip was an eager participant in the Spanish Inquisition that had burned thousands of heretics at the stake, and Protestants were defined as heretics.

"Mass for me on Sunday," howled Elizabeth. "Humiliation today and every day. Northumberland's rooms at Beauchamp Tower, and eventually the scaffold."

Mrs. Ashley watched Elizabeth and then approached her again. "Elizabeth, my dearie." She looked around at the gathered attendants, as if judging which among them might be the spy who would carry the tale of this rant to Mary. "Let us go to your rooms to talk of this matter."

"Look!" Princess Elizabeth fumbled at a large ornament that hung at her waist. Pull at it though she would, it would not come loose. At last, she tore the green silk and gold trim of her gown, ripped the shreds of fabric from the pin, and held the piece aloft on the palm of her beautiful, long-fingered hand. The jewel was a porcelain miniature, set in a gold brooch and decorated with diamonds and rubies.

"Look," Elizabeth said again, scowling around at her household, her voice dampened by despair. "She has commanded me always to wear it. This . . . this portrait of King Henry and *Catherine of Aragon*."

Iris shrank against the wall. If Princess Elizabeth herself was powerless, what of herself?

Elizabeth handed the jewel to Mrs. Ashley with a shudder. Kate put it in her pocket.

"What shall become of me?" Wiping her eyes, Elizabeth allowed Mrs. Ashley to put one arm around her shoulder. They walked away together toward the princess's rooms.

Despair seized Iris. Once again, Elizabeth had dragged her into danger. "And us?" she said, turning to Andrew. "What shall become of us all?"

EIGHTEEN

Five days later, as August came in and London sizzled, King Edward VI was buried at Westminster. Princess Elizabeth did not require Iris, as Queen Mary required Elizabeth, to attend the private funeral mass in Mary's chapel. Iris did not have to see the boy's casket garlanded with white roses or watch his half sisters, princess and queen, and his councilors mourning him.

Grateful for this dispensation, Iris sat in the small garden near the front entry of Somerset House, listening to a linnet sing and reading a green leather book of Petrarch's sonnets she had found in the library. She looked for the bird in the cherry tree above her head, but could not find him or his nest among the leaves. The cherries had already ripened and been eaten by birds and men. Idly, Iris turned to the front of the book of poems. The flyleaf bore an inscription to its owner.

To my dear Uncle Somerset, from your loving nephew
King Edward VI

Somerset had been Edward's lord protector. In happier days, he had even been "dear," yet he had come to the executioner's chopping block by order of the boy king who once had loved him. How ironic it was that Northumberland, who had organized Somerset's death, should await his own execution now.

Iris tried to feel triumph, but she could not.

So many dead.

Having read the inscription in the book, she could no longer see the sonnets for the tears in her eyes. Her emotions fluttered this way and that, like a rag in the wind. In such unsteady circumstances, how could her feelings be stable?

Across the garden, under an old apple tree, Mallory leaned against a low branch and made it bounce her gently, as Sir Jeremy stood looking down at her and talking. Mallory turned away, laughing musically. Was that a blush? Mallory? Blushing in the shadows? Iris smiled. At the age of thirty, Mallory was falling in love. Elizabeth would go wild when she heard: if she was not in love and married, her ladies must not be, either.

Before suppertime, Elizabeth returned from the funeral to Somerset House, red-eyed and silent, her face distorted, as if self-control were an effort too much to bear. Kate Ashley had also remained at home. She must have heard the horses or seen them through a window, for she met the princess at the door. Kate took her by the hand and led her inside. Iris followed them at a discreet distance.

". . . crucifix and statues and incense!" the princess cried out. "King Edward himself ordered such folderol banished from churches. Now, at his *funeral,* Mary's Catholic priest sings the mass that Edward forbade. Day by day, she undoes all that our brother believed in and hoped for." Elizabeth strode up and down the room, shaking her fists. "She watches and waits for her moment, Kate. Mary will have her revenge on me as well, just you watch!"

"My dear," Kate said, in a voice that would have soothed a torrent. "How dreadful that you must submit to Mary's demands. How brave you are."

"Not only to her demands, Kate. Her religion as well," Elizabeth growled. "No matter what I do, the Protestants will soon rise up against her in my name, and I shall be dead, maggoty meat."

Elizabeth's little terrier had dogged her heels so closely that, when she turned suddenly, she stepped on his foot. Skye yelped. The princess swept him up in her arms and held his face to her own, whispering comfort in his ear and tenderly petting him.

Four or five of Elizabeth's other attendants who had gathered at the edge of the room muttered to each other. "Would that she cared as much for us," said Lettice to Margaret. So they were disillusioned with the princess also. Perhaps they too wished to be away from the royal pomp and bitterness, and back at their fathers' estates, like Iris.

Mallory came to Iris's side. "We were safer in the country, pursued by Northumberland's men," she said in a low voice. "Hiding at Linnetwood, or hiding at the Ladle, or hiding at Hatfield."

"Mmm," Iris murmured.

"Bolt-holes and brush piles there were easier to find. We are rather more visible in the queen's finely appointed rooms. Hinds in an open field, we are, our breasts bare to the arrows."

Iris agreed, but she was afraid to say so. She had spoken too frankly to Andrew. For her own protection, she must keep her views to herself. "I only wish that I had some clean clothes," she said. "My gowns grow dingier by the day. I must stay in my room one day and wash away the horse sweat and road dust, or I shall smell like the Tower moat."

Iris leaned against the cool stone wall and watched Elizabeth, one troubled orphan observing another. A wave of pity for the princess moved Iris. "At least I had my mother through my childhood. At least my father loved me."

"I doubt Anne Boleyn would have been much of a mother, even had she lived," Mallory said. "Too selfish. And more years might not have done much good," she added. "Kate Ashley is as close to a mother as Elizabeth ever had."

"Come," Elizabeth called. "No need to stand about here by the door. Come to my rooms. We shall cast off grief with music."

She nodded to Andrew, who stood guard. "Keep the gentlemen away tonight. I want only the company of my ladies." Turning to them, she said, "I am too tired for men's flirtatious games."

No Andrew, then. In fact, Iris had not been able to speak with him alone since Mary's entrance into London. What was this unusual emotion Iris felt? Her disappointment about Andrew's absence surprised her. Her cheeks burned hot. Soon she would become as foolish as Mallory, rocking and laughing by the apple tree.

Iris and the other women, young and old, followed Princess Elizabeth up the broad stone stairs and through the rooms to her reception hall.

Elizabeth was already there, struggling with her sleeves, when Iris entered the room. "Help me out of this loathsome gown," said the princess. While Elizabeth shook out her hair and let it fall to her shoulders, Mrs. Ashley untied the princess's plain black bodice from the undecorated satin sleeves, removed them, and put them across the back of a chair.

"Mary has imprisoned Robert Dudley with his father, along with his other sons. My Robin—Mary knows I love him." Elizabeth spat the words. All at once, she ripped off her skirt and tore it. She tore it again, and again, a cyclone of destruction. Shreds of silk hung in the air like ravens' feathers, before they slowly floated to the floor.

Elizabeth swept up the pieces in her hands and held them to her face. "Mary's clothes grow more gaudy by the day, despite Edward's death! Even her mourning clothes are garish. Onyx. Huge carbuncle garnets. Huge! At our brother's funeral! And pearls—oh, pearls were a crust across her breast."

Iris had never witnessed such a tirade in her life. She looked on, horrified, as Elizabeth hurled the shreds of black silk away from her, but she could not disentangle herself from them. "'Sing a song of blackbirds,'" Elizabeth called out, "'baked in a pie.'" She laughed then, but her laughter contained no humor. Such laughter might have issued from the mouth of a madwoman.

"Mallory," said Mrs. Ashley, her voice calm, "bring Princess Elizabeth's lavender gown." Kate moved Elizabeth to a chair. Under the gentle pressure of Kate's hands, the princess sat down, and Kate began to brush her hair.

Shrinking against the wall, Iris hoped not to be noticed. Mallory returned with a gown made of wool, gossamer light, dyed lavender, lined with creamy satin, and placed it over Elizabeth's shoulders. The princess stood and turned her back to the others. Mrs. Ashley, who had clothed her and disrobed her since she was a small child, helped her out of her undergarments—the whalebone frame that made a gown stand out from a woman's body, the voluminous petticoats, the drawers, the fine linen chemise, the knitted silk stockings. One by one, she folded each garment and placed it with the others.

Fastening her gown, Elizabeth turned back to her ladies. Iris moved behind Lettice and made herself small, hiding as the princess sucked all the air from the room. The deceptions and rancor and terror of this place would kill Iris yet. She must ask Elizabeth again to let her go.

Yet Iris admired what she saw. Lavender had never looked so lovely as it did now, played against the princess's red curls.

When she wore a russet dress or gold, her eyes were hazel; when she was dressed in green, her eyes were green pools; at this moment, they seemed almost black. Barefoot, she sat down at her virginals, opened its handpainted, ivory-inlaid cover, and let her fingers trip over the ivory keys. The song, one Iris's mother had played, wrung her heart.

"Light the candles in this gloomy old house," Elizabeth commanded, her voice shrill. "My father's third wife's eldest brother was good for something. Give thanks to Somerset, that we have a roof over our heads!" She turned back to the ladies as she played. "Dance! Order our supper to be served here, Kate. Dance, my ladies!"

Lady Lettice and Lady Margaret rolled up the reed floor covering against the walls, and the ladies obeyed. The music was complicated, yet Elizabeth played it from memory, with no hesitation or lapse of confidence. When she finished the song, she stood up from the bench. "Now you, Mallory. You play."

Elizabeth moved Lettice aside and seized Iris's cold hand in her warm one. Even if she tried, Iris could not hide.

"Take off your slippers, lest you tread on my naked toes and make me yelp like Skye," said Elizabeth. Iris removed her kidskin slippers and threw them into the corner. "Now dance."

Mallory played a song Iris had never heard before, its pace increasing until it was nearly frenzied. All the other women joined Elizabeth and Iris, turning and whirling and leaping into the air as high as they could. Iris had heard of this athletic dance. Country people who traveled to the capital and returned to Linnet-upon-Byrne reported Londoners' fantastic diversions, clucking their tongues. Sometimes, they said, the dancers fell; sometimes they broke bones. Once, Iris had heard, a dancer even leapt and whirled himself right down a stone staircase and died of a broken neck. Perhaps he had drunk too much wine, people said, but now Iris thought that a man well might lose his head in this dance, intoxicated merely by the frenzy, might even die of elation.

The dance was a strange imitation of life in a palace, Iris thought, each dancer striving alone for herself, each out of touch with the others and trying to avoid collision, each struggling to survive. Iris was gasping for air, angry that Elizabeth continued as if she had just begun to dance, oblivious to the needs of any but herself. When would Mallory's song end? But Mallory was watching the princess, gauging the length of the song to Elizabeth's energy, while the others struggled to keep up. Elizabeth's stamina would kill them all!

When at last the princess nodded and Mallory ended the song, the ladies all sank to the floor in a heap, leaning against each other, laughing and panting.

"My feet!" groaned Lady Lettice. "I shall never walk again."

"Take off your slippers, as *I* do," said Elizabeth, laughing at her ladies' weakness. "Run up and down stairs as *I* do every morning to build your strength. Bathe in icy water."

Iris stood at Elizabeth's side, catching her breath, wishing she could disappear in fact, as she had faded to nothing in the princess's perceptions. How little sympathy the princess showed for people less robust than herself.

"Come sit by me."

Oh, now Iris was visible again. Elizabeth must have need of her. They sat down on large tapestry cushions of eiderdown, placed on the floor far enough away from the virginals that the two could hear each other's conversation, although Mallory began to play again and the ladies continued to dance.

"I need strong people about me, lest Mary grind me down. People strong of character to help me keep strong," said Elizabeth, when she was settled with Skye at her side. "You heard what Mary has done. Agree to stay, Iris."

Elizabeth persisted in the pretense that Iris had choices, when in fact they both knew she had none. Elizabeth wanted obedience in the guise of willing service. Iris's courage had seeped away since the day she blew a kiss to Northumberland. Now she bowed her head, looking for strength, as if she could find it in her lap. Elizabeth's wild moods terrified her, this calmness no less than her earlier frenzy. No wonder Mother and Lucy had counseled steadiness to Iris.

She found the strength to answer the princess. She must ask to be released. "I am honored," she said. "'Tis a great thing to live in your presence, but I do love the simple life."

"I shall ask Mary to restore your inheritance to you," said Elizabeth, "if you will stand by me."

Linnetwood. Iris's heart's desire was offered, but with a catch. Why couldn't Iris just accept, bide her time, see whether Elizabeth would keep her word? Had Iris the patience, she might return to her home its mistress. No. Not even for Linnetwood could she submit to the tyrant princess and pretend to like the role of slave.

"Much as I should like your company, your Highness, the English countryside calls my heart." Iris watched the dancers leap and whirl, and weighed her words. "London is not a place for me."

Elizabeth pleated the fine wool of her lavender gown between her fingers, but she watched Iris intently. Iris must guard her ears, lest she lose them to Elizabeth's whim, like the hind in the water.

"We shall spend as much time in the country as Mary allows," said Elizabeth. "I have asked her to let me return to Hatfield."

Iris avoided Elizabeth's eyes. "Hatfield is lovely. Linnetwood is home."

"But you have nothing to return to. Your father's title and estate reverted to the crown."

"Yes," said Iris. "So you have reminded me. I know the story well, since it is my own. The king settled my father's lands on Northumberland."

"And now they are Mary's." Elizabeth blew through pursed lips, her patience evidently wearing thin. "Then where would you go?"

"While the estate now is Queen Mary's, the land has not disappeared into her treasury, nor the house, nor the people. Let me return there."

"How?" Elizabeth's exasperation bubbled out with every little word.

"I shall milk the cows. Gather the eggs. Serve the old stableman who once served me."

"Ohhh, Iris—" Now Elizabeth's voice was shrill. Despite

the music, the ladies turned to look as they danced. "Remaining here, you shall see your revenge come to Northumberland."

Elizabeth had played this chess piece before. Since the time when she begged Iris to decoy Northumberland's men, Iris realized now, she had grown beyond Elizabeth's lure. "Revenge is no longer my reason to live."

"Good. Revenge has little meat on its bones. But I could give you wealth and station," Elizabeth insisted. "Mary is not well. Should I survive to inherit her crown, you shall be among the greatest in my realm, attending the Queen of England when Mary is dead."

Elizabeth the chess player waited, but Iris did not respond to the ploy of power and glory. She had seen enough of court. The princess seized her hand, and dropped her voice to a hoarse whisper. "Stay with me! Please."

Here came the strategy most likely to win Iris over, an appeal from a person who was merely a young woman in need, but Iris would not let Elizabeth's blandishments draw her into servitude again. "I want to return to Linnetwood."

Elizabeth leaned back and plumped one of the beautiful cushions. Against a red background, a needlepoint unicorn lay under a tree, surrounded by a fence. The fence was low; the unicorn could easily have freed itself.

"Ah, Iris. You wish to return to Linnetwood, and I desire nothing more than my return to Hatfield. Home calls us both, but as my dear Kate reminds me daily, even hourly sometimes, we must accept our fate."

"You devise my fate, for better or for worse," said Iris. She could hardly hear her own words for the pounding in her head. Her stubbornness was rash, she knew. While Elizabeth might appreciate the idea of an independent mind, she would tolerate no original thoughts about the rights of underlings and the privileges of royalty.

Elizabeth laughed. "As stubborn as myself, you are! I have to credit you. You are even more pigheaded than I thought." She picked up Skye, fluffed his ears, and stood.

Iris stood, too.

"If you go, I shall make your life miserable, you know," said Elizabeth.

"I shall be sorry for that. I should never wish to leave you without your blessing, your Highness, but I do desire with all my heart to return to Linnetwood."

"Leave me." Elizabeth's voice was a low growl. "Return my gown to Kate Ashley tonight. She will house you with the other servants. You shall eat in the kitchen and clean the hearths for your keep. If you wish to be a milkmaid, you shall do so here."

Now Iris had lost the flimsy support of Elizabeth's unreliable goodwill along with everything else. Soon Iris would have to run away, but, at the moment, she felt so weak she could hardly stand.

Princess Elizabeth turned her back. With a flip of her hair, she strode away. "Dance," she shouted as she passed the dancing ladies. "Faster! Dance, damn you!"

NINETEEN

Iris went to her room and looked down at the beautiful gardens of Somerset House. She removed Elizabeth's iridescent dress before Mrs. Ashley could ask her to do so. She drew the blue gown out from under the mattress, where she had hidden it for safekeeping as soon as she arrived at Somerset House, put it on, and waited for instructions.

Suppertime came and went. Iris sat at her window and watched boats pass up and down the Thames below the gardens. The birds went to their beds, and the sun set. Iris took her last taper and went through the dark halls down to the kitchen for something to eat.

"May I have a bit of bread and milk?" she asked Cook, who was checking her stores in preparation for tomorrow's meals.

Cook cut two slabs of fine white bread, buttered them thickly, and spread them with strawberry jam. She put them on a pewter plate, and put the plate on a tray with a mug of milk. "Some cheese, my lady?"

Iris nodded. "Thank you. Has anybody mentioned my helping you here?" The aged cheese smelled delicious.

Cook laughed as she added an apple to the tray. "Now, what would my fine lady be doing here in the heat and bustle?"

Iris smiled at her. "I thought I might like to learn some baking."

"You keep to your place, and I'll keep to mine," Cook said. "Nothing freezes my nerves more than to have the high and mighty looking over my shoulder."

Now Iris belonged nowhere. Though hardly able to walk, weighed down as she was with that knowledge, she lit the taper with a brand from the hearth. She set the light on the tray, which she carried back to the room where she had stayed since coming to Somerset House. As Iris ate, she read the green leather book of Petrarch's sonnets by the flickering candlelight. The verses contrasted acts of love with acts of duty, concluding that the best acts were those of loving duty or dutiful love.

Iris shut the book hard. She had had enough of preaching.

Still nobody came to direct her to a room in the servants' quarters. The low voices of men walking on the graveled path below floated to the window, but she could not make out their words. The moon had risen, adding its light to that of the candle, now burned halfway down. Iris opened the desk and wrote a note to Thorpe with the goose quill she found there among the fine parchment. She was well, she wrote; though she wished to return home, she must await the will of the princess; and how was he? Though Thorpe could not read, Simon or James would read the letter for him and take down his reply. Iris held a stick of red sealing wax in the candle flame, dripped the molten liquid on the folded letter, and used the bottom of the pottery mug to press the seal thin. While it was still soft, she etched her initials in the wax with a little knife she found.

The men on the path under Iris's window went inside. The candle burned low. The moon climbed to the top of the sky. The scent of the climbing roses that bloomed outside her window perfumed the whole room. Other people passed below, but this time the voices were those of women. A small dog barked. Skye.

Iris doused the candle and looked out the open window. Elizabeth. Yes, there was Skye, running around the two ladies again and again. Elizabeth and Mrs. Ashley, out for a walk in the garden. The dancing must be over. Nothing stopped the princess, not even the fear of disease caused by night vapors, a fear that kept all but the most reckless people inside after dark. Having grown up in the country, like Iris, she listened to her own experience rather than the superstitions of the mob.

The two women mounted the steps, followed by the terrier, and reentered the house.

Surely now Mrs. Ashley would come and tell Iris where to sleep. She waited in the dark for her instructions, but nobody came. So she removed her mother's dress and slipped her nightdress over her head. Perhaps Elizabeth had thought better of her threat. No, surely not; the princess was not the apologetic sort. She would wait until morning to banish Iris to the servants' hall.

Iris dreamed of horsemen pursuing her. She dreamed of the scaffold on Tower Green. The headsman waited for her, masked, leaning on the handle of his ax. Something was new in this night's dream: this time Iris smiled at the executioner, turned her back on him, and walked out through the Tower gate, which opened at her approach.

When morning came and the robins that nested among the climbing roses and clematis woke her, Iris got up with deeper purpose than she had felt in months. She was but a girl of fifteen. With no advocates, no title or property, no money, no male protector, she was hardly more than chattel, Queen Mary's ward. If she returned to Linnetwood against Elizabeth's and Mary's will, Thorpe and her other old friends could not take her in without risk to themselves. She had no choice but to serve the princess. While the Tudors controlled the whereabouts of her body, however, her mind was her own place.

This realization jolted her to the bone.

Here in Princess Elizabeth's house on the river, although Iris awaited the princess's pleasure, she had learned to heed Mrs. Ashley's advice in her own way. She owned her own spirit at last, wherever she might live. Accepting what she must, she was oddly free.

As Iris pondered and waited, a serving maid brought her breakfast again, as if the acrimony of the previous evening had never happened. Iris dressed herself and ate. And read. And paced. And waited some more.

The rap Iris dreaded finally came. "Come in."

"Good morning, dear." The visitor was Mrs. Ashley. Though Iris had already pulled up the covers and made her bed neat, Kate nervously smoothed and plucked at nonexistent wrinkles. "She wants you in her rooms. You mustn't hold her last night's temper against her, Iris. She hardly knows which way to look, for fear of what Mary will do."

"I can easily imagine such fear, subject as I am to Elizabeth's whim." Fire snapped in Iris's voice.

"Your position is hardly the same; Mary hates her," Mrs. Ashley snapped back. "People are talking of Mary's burning Protestants at the stake. Elizabeth must guard her every word and act. Now come."

Chastened, Iris followed her through one room after another, down one stone staircase and up another. She would never learn the arrangement of these millions of rooms. Mrs. Ashley stopped her with a signal and went on alone. In a moment, Mrs. Ashley returned and beckoned Iris forward.

The princess was still dressed in the previous night's clothing, the lavender wool and cream silk gown, but she was no longer barefoot. She wore creamy silk stockings now, and ermine slippers covered her feet, the fur turned inside and the leather embroidered with purple thistles and pink roses. Lavender wells shadowed her eyes, and her skin was pale, her long white fingers tremulous. Perhaps she hadn't slept. Strain was not kind to Princess Elizabeth's beauty. Iris curtsied. She would not tremble; she would not weep, or bow down her head, no matter what happened, for this time she was not weak.

"You look tired, Iris," said Elizabeth. "Nor did I sleep, either. Rise, and sit."

Iris did as she was ordered. "I wish us both peace and easy sleep, madam."

"Ha. You may come to such riches, but I shan't have them in this lifetime." Skye leapt into Elizabeth's lap and nosed her neck. Elizabeth shook her head and sighed. "Nobody and nothing can make me more secure than I am at this moment, no more than Mary decrees."

Iris looked down at her hands, clasped in her lap. "Would that you were safe, Princess."

"Would that I were, indeed. You know, Iris, most ladies long for such a high place in the world as I offer you. For most people, power is irresistible. Splendor and money, too. Yet you desire them not."

"Who in her right mind would wish to share the insecurity you describe, your Highness?"

Elizabeth sighed. "Quite right. My ladies must be mad. Or they must love me. Tell me again what you desire above all else."

"I desire to return to Linnetwood."

"You do not wish to toast Northumberland's execution with me?"

Iris thought again of the deer's sacrificial ear. "No, my lady, I beg your pardon, but I do not. I thought I wanted nothing more. Now I see I was mistaken."

"You say you would go to Linnetwood as a servant?"

"I would."

"Very well. You shall have your heart's desire, Iris."

Iris looked up at Elizabeth's face. Was the princess teasing her?

"I am practicing modesty and restraint, as Kate advises me," Elizabeth went on. "I spoke about you to Queen Mary some days ago, when first we met in London."

Elizabeth nervously petted her little dog. "She knows what service you performed, drawing Northumberland's men, keeping them off balance. His men scattered everywhere, you know, searching for you, thinking they searched for me. Mary knows you divided their forces, at risk of death."

Iris was holding her breath, waiting for what would happen next, unable to hope or wish or fear or think beyond this moment.

"In recognition of your service, and at my request, Mary has nullified the seizure of your father's estate and title. As his heir, Iris, the estate is yours. And Mary has made you Countess of Bentham."

For all her determination to hide her feelings, Iris trembled. She wept. She knelt at the feet of Elizabeth Tudor.

"Up. Up, I say!" Elizabeth said. "No more groveling today."

Iris sat again, as straight and proud as possible, and tried to speak, but shock had taken her voice.

"Yes. You want to know whether you must stay in London. Last night, I did hope you would remain with me, but I have no need of those who wish to be away," said Elizabeth. "You shall leave my house immediately. Sir Andrew shall accompany you and guarantee your safety."

Overcome with the sudden change in her fortune, Iris nevertheless found her voice. "I shall come again, if you have need of me, so long as I am free to go."

"Go *now*, Iris, before I change my mind. I have worse things to worry about."

Curtsying, Iris backed through the doorway. She ran through the galleries, skipped down the stone steps, danced up the other staircase, taking two steps at a time. In her own room she flung herself on her bed and realized that she was wearing nearly all that she had brought from home. She had nothing to gather up, except for this letter to Thorpe she had left on the bed, sealed with red wax in which she had scratched her initials. She need only roll up her nightdress. She could leave. She was going home.

Mrs. Ashley had followed. She smiled at the door. She was saying something:

". . . and Sir Andrew has your horse in the stableyard."

"Is he to stay with me at Linnetwood—Andrew, I mean?"

"I gather, from the stories I hear, he would stay wherever you might be, my dear," said Mrs. Ashley. "But Princess Elizabeth would not give him up."

Iris tucked her letter to Thorpe into her bodice. She

would deliver it personally. Now Andrew waited for her in the stableyard. She would stop at Mrs. Pennefeather's for her mother's fur-lined cape and her father's signet ring. Linnetwood waited for her at the end of her journey, and Edward Thorpe. Robinson would be there too, and James, and Cook, and Simon. She might even see Adam again, the boy she had kissed under the arbor all those months ago, if he was not yet married. And though Andrew would return to London, his departure would not be forever, Iris was sure.

Iris kissed Mrs. Ashley on one cheek, and then the other, and then her forehead and chin. "Good-bye," she said. "Thank you."

"Not good-bye," said Kate Ashley. "Only farewell for now. We shall meet again, I am certain. A countess may not stay away from court forever."

"Yes," said Iris, thinking how small a world was England, how everyone's fate crossed everyone else's, how one surprise opened into another. "I doubt it not."

Then Iris, the genuine mistress of Linnetwood, picked up the skirts of her mother's favorite gown and ran down the back stairs of Somerset House to the stableyard, where her dear friend Andrew waited to escort her home.

Afterword

Like all historical novels, this story is a mixture of fact and fiction. The turmoil following King Edward's death is factual. The Duke of Northumberland did try to transfer the crown from the Tudors to his own family, and some historians think that it was William Cecil who warned Princess Elizabeth and Princess Mary about the plot to lure them to London and their probable execution. Katherine Ashley did, in fact, attend Elizabeth from her early childhood.

Iris and her family, and Elizabeth's knights and other ladies, are fictional, as is Iris's role as counterfeit princess. However, a young noblewoman in that turbulent time might have played such a part.

Once she was in power, Queen Mary executed Northumberland, as well as his son, Lord Guildford Dudley, and Lady Jane Grey. Robert Dudley, Elizabeth's childhood friend, was spared. When Mary died only five years later, Elizabeth ascended the throne. She appointed William Cecil Secretary of State, her principal adviser. He and Katherine Ashley served Queen Elizabeth the rest of their lives. Elizabeth reigned from 1558 to 1603 and became the greatest monarch in English history.

Jane Resh Thomas has written more than a dozen fiction and nonfiction books for young readers. Her books for Clarion include the award-winning *Behind the Mask: The Life of Queen Elizabeth I* and *The Princess in the Pigpen*, a time-travel story set in the Elizabethan period. She also teaches in the MFA Program in Writing for Children and Young Adults at Vermont College.

Ms. Thomas lives in Minneapolis, Minnesota.